Trans Wizard Harriet Porber And The Bad Boy Parasaurolophus

An Adult Romance Novel

CHUCK TINGLE

You prove love is real.

- Chuck Tingle

CONTENTS

ACKNOWLEDGMENTS

Thank you, dear reader, for speaking up and letting your voice and your truth ring out against the powers of The Void.

ONE HIT WONDER

1

Inspiration can be hard to find for a woman like me, but it's not without trying.

When I look out the window of my modest Brooklyn apartment, I see that the world happening all around me is beautiful, and strange, and special, but for some reason that just won't translate into excitement. I'm a wizard by trade, and you'd think that means I can cast any spell I want, but unfortunately that's not the case. I need to be *excited* about something if I'm gonna put my wand in the air.

It's always been this way, and between you and me, I'd call this my secret weapon. This is how I managed to develop a full-fledged wizarding career without any previous experience in the spells and magic industry, how my first spell, *Bubblus Morphus,* managed to explode into a viral sensation the likes of which nobody has ever seen.

Sure, it was nothing more than a simple collection of magical bubbles containing various scenes from the caster's life, but it was easy to personalize and the scroll soon went viral. I'm proud of that spell.

I only spellcraft when I'm passionate to spellcraft, and because of that, I can only create magical effects with true, breathtaking, potent, bleeding, honest heart and soul.

Then again, since graduating wizard school I've only published one hit spell.

I've been sitting here staring out the window of my apartment for days now, my eyes following the men in suits on their way to work, the young guys playing basketball in the park across the street and the woman shouting into a megaphone on the corner. They've all got their own important stories to tell, and I know this, but they aren't *my* story.

That's what a hit spell does: tells a good story about the wizard who crafted it.

These people won't inspire me to create the follow up that I need for a first original spell that was so sizzling hot, the very prospect of another one like it seems to make people scoff and roll their eyes.

Even worse, it makes those in the spellcrafting industry smirk to themselves, excited to watch me crash and burn when the world proves that lightening doesn't strike twice.

I adjust my glasses uncomfortably.

Ironically, when I wrote my first spell I was in a similar place, fresh off a new breakup and deeply questioning whether or not I would ever be able to trust again.

After *Bubblus Morphus* came out I was thrust into the spotlight, although it wasn't exactly the brightest spotlight because the wizarding world only matters so much compared to the twinkling stars of Hollywood or the intellectualized pursuit of book publishing. This brief flash of fame brought about all kinds of suitors, and soon enough that hole inside of me was filled by a man who I thought I could trust, but ended up being just as bad as the guys before him.

Suddenly, there's a loud hum that causes me to jump in my seat. I glance down at my phone as it vibrates across the desk, immediately recognizing the number of my apartment front door buzzer. I have no idea who this could be, but the mystery itself suddenly makes the answer abundantly clear. There's only one person who would show up in the middle of the afternoon like this, unannounced, the one person who has been riding my back lately, even more concerned about the next spell than I am.

"Hello?" I answer, putting the caller on speakerphone.

"You writing yet?" comes the familiar voice of my spellcraft agent.

"Yes, Minerma, I'm just about finished. Only a few more magical incantations and you've got yourself another hit," I tell her flatly.

There's a long pause on the other end of the line, the silence hanging between us while Minerma's mind races. She's well aware of my dry sarcasm, and she should know better by now, but she's also clearly blinded but the faint prospect of real steps being made towards a follow up spell.

"Are you serious?" my agent finally questions.

"No," I tell her bluntly.

Another moment of silence hangs in the air between us.

"Do you want to come up?" I finally ask with a laugh.

I don't even wait for an answer, pressing the keypad on my phone and instantly hearing my apartment's front door open through the speakers with a loud, rattling clank. Footsteps come softly clicking up my staircase and seconds later there's a short, staccato knock at my door.

Minerma is hilarious. She's been here hundreds of times now, and we're about as close as a spellcraft agent and wizard can get, yet her timid nature won't even allow her to enter my home without knocking first. She's prim and proper, the opposite of a sorcerer like myself.

"You know you can just come right in," I call out.

The door opens slightly and Minerma pokes her head out from the crack. "What?"

"I said you can just come in," I laugh. "I've told you this a thousand times."

The spellcraft agent nods and steps into my apartment living room, dressed in a well-tailored suit and skirt combination that's just inches away from being stylish but not quite getting there thanks to the drab coloring and conservative hemline.

"I know, I know," Minerma assures me, "but this is your space as a *wizard*. I don't want to disrupt that."

My agent takes the world of magic very seriously, due to the fact that she's a complete and utter outsider here. I'd go so far as to say that there's not a single mystical bone in Minerma's body, not as a slight, but as an honest assessment of her character. She probably couldn't even handle one of those single spell wands with a little magic trick made for children.

The thing is, Minerma clearly loves magic and sorcery, and as a fan she's made it quite far in the world of spellcrafting. She knows well enough to give her wizards what they want, but sometimes she can take things overboard.

"Don't worry, I haven't been crafting," I offer. "I've just been staring out my window for…" I trail off, then pick up my phone and check the hour.

Moments later, I realize that the time of day still isn't gonna cut it, then make a note of the date. "Three weeks," I finally state, bluntly. "I haven't written a word of this spell in three weeks."

Minerma just stares at me, her mind racing but her expression staying completely stoic. She knows that I like to fuck with her.

"Harriet, are you serious?" my agent questions.

I nod.

"What happened to those ten pages of incantations you were working on," Minerma continues, trying to hide her deep concern.

"No good," I admit. "I deleted them."

My agent's eyes go wide. "Why would you do that? I didn't even get a chance to read them!"

"No good," I repeat, shaking my head from side to side. "They were just… filler, there wasn't any heart to the spell. The words sounded okay when you slid them up next to each other, but nothing behind them mattered."

Minerma lets out a long sigh, trusting the process. "Alright, alright. Just remember, the longer it takes for us to get your next spell out, the more interest starts to die."

I'm a little shocked when my friend says this. She's utterly terrified to disrupt the creative process, and yet somehow bringing up the shelf life of my fame is fair game. This is unlike her.

"You're pressuring me," I remind Minerma. "That's just going to make things worse. Us wizards need space for new ideas to bloom. You're in my garden, Minerma. You're trampling all the little flowers as they try to poke their heads out of the dirt. They're so small and pretty and you're just stomping through with your big boots, not even looking."

I expect to get a smile out of this from my spellcraft agent but she remains completely straight faced. "You're not hearing me," Minerma tries again. "I'm saying the longer it takes, the more *interest* starts to die."

"You're just saying the same thing," I inform my friend. "Those are literally the same words."

Minerma hesitates a bit longer and then finally cracks, her expression shifting to one of frustrated defeat. She walks over to the nearby couch and flops down onto it, her body going from a typically rigid stance to one of utter relaxation.

"I shouldn't be telling you this," my agent starts, "because the company wants to be very careful with how they handle things moving forward."

"I'm listening," I reply.

"You know that we have a new head wizard at Morgan Phoenix Spellcrafting, right?" Minerma questions.

"You mentioned that," I offer. "You also mentioned how it didn't matter in the slightest."

"Turns out, it does," my agent continues. "Hank, the new head wizard, he's going to clean house soon. Nothing has happened yet, but every day we're having meetings about what wizards and bards and warlocks are headed to the chopping block next; who we can afford to keep and who we can afford to lose."

Suddenly, a flicker of panic bubbles up within me. I try my best to stay calm and push it away, but there's no denying the fact that it's there. I'm usually relaxed enough to let these kinds of things wash over me, understanding that everything will work itself out in the end, but seeing Minerma's terrified expression has put me on edge. She's usually so good about maintaining a professional air, and this break in character signifies something powerful brewing behind the scenes.

"I wrote your best-selling spell of last year," I remind her. "There's no way any of this applies to me."

"Three years," Minerma counters.

"What?" I question, confused.

"You wrote the best-selling spell of the year *three years* ago," my agent clarifies. "It's been longer than you think. I know you were the top of your class at wizarding school, and I know you had a pretty big hit spell after that... but it's been a while now."

I close my eyes and try to remember that moment when I walked over to the magic store and picked up a freshly printed copy of *Bubblus Morphus,* unfurling the exceptionally long scroll with a deep breath as the intoxicating scent of new spell filled my nostrils. There's no way that was over a year ago, I think to myself, but the longer I focus on this memory, the more I start to realize that time has been passing a lot faster than I thought.

"So what?" I finally blurt. "Two years go by and people start to forget about you?"

Minerma doesn't react.

"Seriously?" I question.

My spellcraft agent shrugs. "You've got a lot of fans who are anxious for a follow up, but the realm of hot-to-trot magic is a difficult genre. There's so much of it out there, and if you're not releasing things consonantly, your fans tend to move on to something new."

"My spell's not hot-to-trot!" I counter. "It's more like… memory magic."

This has long been a point of contention between the spellcrafting company and me, a battle that I was eventually forced to surrender. I've always considered *Bubblus Morphus* to be piece of serious sorcery with hot-to-trot undertones, but the folks in business suits see things differently. I suppose I should be thankful that they do, because my spell was a massive genre hit, but it's something that I still find myself dwelling on.

"Whatever you want to call it is fine," Minerma continues. "It still needs a follow up. Listen, you know that I'm on your side in all this, you know that I want the best for you as a wizard, but you need to start crafting again."

I don't protest. I'm aware of all this, and just as frustrated with my own wizard's block as Minerma is.

"Besides, your fans aren't the problem. The problem is that our new head wizard wants to see forward momentum. Everything he's in the process of cutting is being dropped to make room for the future, and three years ago might as well be twenty to him. He's trying to shape things in his image, which means there needs to be a new project in the works from you," my agent explains. "You need fresh words."

"Well, what am I supposed to do?" I suddenly blurt, frustrated. "I'm sitting up here trying to find inspiration but it's all the same shit outside my window every day! This is where I crafted *Bubblus Morphus* from start to finish, you'd think there'd be so mojo left in this old wooden desk."

"Maybe that's the problem," my agent offers. "Maybe you need a change of scenery."

"Where can I go?" I question. "I love my parents, but it's not like I have any space to work when I visit them. I don't have a vacation home to go to."

"I have one," Minerma interrupts.

I stare at her blankly, suddenly trying to calculate exactly how much one makes as a wizarding agent. I'm the one with the record-breaking bestseller, but Minerma's got the vacation home?

"Really?" I finally ask.

Minerma nods. "I mean, it belonged to my parents, now it belongs to me. Have you ever heard of the Tingler Islands?"

I shake my head, suddenly dreaming of swaying palm trees and beautiful white sand beaches. "It sounds tropical."

"It's not," my agent replies with a laugh, "but it's secluded, and it's definitely a change of scenery. I think it'd be hard *not* to find inspiration there. The cabin is on Portork Island, part of the Tinglers. It's right off the coast of England."

"England," I repeat back to Minerma, furrowing my brow. "That's pretty damn far."

"Exactly," she retorts. "I used to spend summers over there. Now that autumn is rolling around the island should be almost completely empty. Just you and nature... plus your laptop and parchments."

"Of course," I offer with a smile.

I turn around and gaze out the window, considering my options. As much as I complain about the monotony of my life at the moment, there's also something incredibly cozy about the fact that I know exactly what's going to happen at any given time. I know where I'm going to get dinner tonight, what it's going to feel like waking up in my own bed every morning.

A change is definitely a good idea, but days, weeks or months spent on a tiny island across the Atlantic Ocean is much more drastic than I was thinking.

"Maybe I'll just go upstate," I offer, my gaze still transfixed on the street below.

The second that I say this, I notice the city bus pull up right on schedule, rolling to a stop and then opening up its doors with a loud, dramatic hiss. I can recognize the bus driver, taking note of the fact that he's drinking his usual order of cold chocolate milk.

Before the passengers have a chance to exit the bus, I rattle off their descriptions under my breath. "Old lady, man with briefcase and blue tie, kid in Yankee's gear carrying a grocery bag."

Moments later, a little old woman climbs down the bus steps carefully, using the railing support until she finds a sturdy footing on the curb. Behind her, the man in the suit nearly bowls her over, rushing off to some important meeting in his light blue, striped tie, and bringing up the rear is the young guy in a Yankee's uniform.

I knew they were coming, because that's just what happens on Tuesday.

"What was that?" Minerma calls over, confused by the fact that I'm now mumbling to myself.

I turn around to look at my friend again. "Maybe I *could* use a change of scenery. How long can I stay at your cabin?"

"If you're spellcrafting, as long as it takes," Minerma replies excitedly.

I smile, trying my best not to let on to the fact that, honestly, I have no idea how much spellcrafting I'll actually accomplish. At this point, I wouldn't be surprised if I never wrote another word, the once overflowing well within my soul completely tapped dry.

That's not gonna stop me from trying though.

DELLATRIX AND BRACO

2

It's pretty incredible just how different islands can be from one another.

Of course, I don't live in Manhattan, but I've spent enough time across the bridge to know what it's like in that madhouse of a city. Cars honking, people screaming at one another in anger and frustration, music blasting from a nearby boom box; these are the sounds that I've grown to know like the back of my hand. I know them so well, in fact, that I don't even seem to notice anymore, the cacophony blending together and creating a warm blanket that's always wrapped tightly around me.

Now, all that I hear is the soft hum of a massive ferryboat that rumbles below my feet, along with the distant call of seagulls echoing across the water.

The breathtaking vista that spreads out before me is unlike anything I have ever seen, a natural beauty that has remained remarkably untouched by human kind over the years. The water is flat and calm, a strange bluish gray hue to the waves that can only be attained when the morning fog is hovering low over the surface. Scattered throughout my field of vision are a variety of tree-covered islands, lush and dark green with rocky beaches that show no trace of footprints or campfires. One of them appears to have an old wooden dock that juts out into the water, but the thing is falling apart and looks like it was abandoned years ago. Now the only ones using this skeletal collection of wooden pilings are the barnacles and starfish that hang from the sides near the water line.

I'm sure there are plenty of times during the year that this ferry is crowded with people, vacationers excited to be spending their warm summer days fishing or hiking through the woods, but the off season is even more empty than I expected.

I begin to walk again, making my way along the outer deck of the ferry. I'm one of the only passengers aboard this massive vessel, and I've got the circular landing completely to myself. This deck stretches all the way around the perimeter of the ship, allowing a complete scenic view of the passing islands from every angle. It's an incredible experience, as long as you're bundled up tight enough for the cold English air.

My long coat flowing around me, I finally arrive at the front of the ship, gazing out across the water towards our eventual destination. I can see the ferry dock edging its way closer and closer in the distance, a small village surrounding the structure and a long road behind that winds up farther into the thick forest.

This is Portork Island, much bigger than the others and home to several thousand residents who come and go throughout the year. Soon enough, it's going to be the birthplace of my next hit spell.

Realizing now that our arrival is drawing near, I decide to head back to my car, parked and waiting on the lower deck. My rental is one of the only vehicles on board, and so far the other passengers remain elusive.

I head back inside the ship and immediately spot two of these tough-to-find fellow riders, chuckling to myself at just how much they stick out like a sore thumb.   This section of the ship serves as both a dining hall and a place for people to lounge, rows and rows of soft green benches lining the sides and facing one another with a table in between. At one of the tables sits two sentient motorcycles, gossiping loudly and laughing at some joke that's, apparently, absolutely hilarious because they are nearly choking on the giggles as they bubble up inside of them.

The motorcycles are clad in flashy designer clothes, a bright red coat hanging off of one of them while the other boasts a puffy, white and gold jacket.

I continue walking, but as I pass the living vehicles their giggles quite down into whispers, clearly taking note of my presence.

"Hey!" one of the motorcycles calls over to me, long dark hair framing her face in frizzy waves, with a patch of stark white on the side. "What's your name?"

I stop and turn back to her. "Harriet."

"Nice shoes," she says with a smile that's just the slightest bit too wide to be sincere. I pick up on her hostility almost immediately, but she's so good at selling her well-meaning expression that it actually gives me pause.

"Oh, thank you," I reply, glancing down to remind myself of the pair that I picked out this morning.

I realize almost immediately that this living motorbike is clearly messing with me. Knowing that I'd be traveling a lot today, I picked out a comfortable pair of ratty old sneakers, slipping them on so that I could easily remove them on the plane early this morning while I caught a few extra hours of sleep.

The motorcycle exchanges glances with her slightly lower horsepower, blonde friend, but neither of them say anything more, just sharing a private joke between one another at my expense.

I turn and continue walking but stop suddenly, my inner New Yorker finally catching up with me. I'm not an aggressive woman, in general, but I'm also not afraid of a fight if someone's looking for one. As a trans person, I haven't always been accepted by those with shitty attitudes and narrow minds, and over the years I've learned to stick up for myself.

"You don't seem like you're from around here," I finally say, turning to face them once more.

The frizzy haired motorcycle in the red coat shakes her head. "Nope. Los Angeles. Bogmorts School for Wizards before that. We worked for the groundskeeper, Magrid."

"What's *your* name?" I question. "I told you mine, you didn't tell me yours."

The sentient motorbike realizes her mistake with such sincerity that I'm suddenly pushed back in the opposite direction, believing that she might've actually been genuine with her initial compliment. "I'm so sorry," she gushes. "I'm Dellatrix and this is Braco."

Braco smiles mischievously. Her perfectly symmetrical face is framed by medium-length, stark blonde hair, while Dellatrix's long dark lock cascade down around her shoulders in fizzy waves, highlighted by a streak of brilliant white. The chrome of their motorcycle bodies is perfectly crafted and beautifully maintained.

The paintjob of Dellatrix features a white streak down her side to match the one on her head, while Braco's is mostly greens and greys.

"It's nice to meet you Dellatrix and Braco," I tell them, still trying to get a read.

"Nice to meet you, Harriet," Braco continues. "I really do love your outfit."

"Thanks," I reply.

"You look so… comfortable," Dellatrix chimes in.

I take a deep breath, still struggling to maintain my composure. I'm here to work on a spell, not get into a fight with two evil motorcycles on the ferry. Regardless, I came into this trip fully prepared to deescalate one or two confrontations. Being from the big city, I tend to assume folks are being less than genuine, and that's caused a few misunderstandings in the past.

The thing is, these motorcycles are from the big city, too.

"What brings you to the island?" I question, attempting to push the conversation elsewhere.

"Oh, we're just visiting a friend," Dellatrix explains.

I nod, then fall into silence again, not quite sure where to take this conversation. Finally, I give up.

"Well, I gotta get back to my car," I tell her.

"Okay," Braco says with a tight-lipped smile and a halfhearted wave, once again lying right on the border between awful and genuine.

I start to walk away, getting no more than ten feet before I hear the motorcycles burst out into another fit of giggles. I stop, briefly considering turning around and launching in on them with a full, Brooklyn-style diatribe, but I somehow manage to restrain myself.

I don't have time for this shit, my clear-headed internal voice reminds the rest of my brain. The sooner I send Minerma my first few spell notes, the sooner I can rest easy, knowing that my spellcrafting deal is safe and secure.

After a deep breath, I collect myself to keep walking.

It's not long before I'm back in the driver's seat of my rental car, staring out at the massive Portork Island ferry dock as our ship continues to close in on it. There are two bigfeet in bright orange vests preparing the ferry for landing, carefully watching over the ship as they go about their docking preparations.

"Last stop, Portork Island. If you have not yet returned to your vehicle then please do so immediately," comes a loud crackling voice over the ferry loudspeaker.

I glance around, seeing that the handful of cars next to me are prepped and waiting, anxious to get off on the island. Only one vehicle remains empty, and I have a good guess who it belongs to.

From the license plate, it appears that this car is also a rental like mine, albeit from a slightly higher income bracket. The thing is absurdly out of place amid this earth-toned scenery, a brilliant yellow two-seater sports car with huge, shimmering silver rims.

A few minutes pass and still, nobody comes to claim the vehicle.

When we finally land and get our instructions to disembark the ferry, the passengers behind this yellow car are force to drive around it, myself included. It's only after I've pulled up onto the main island road that I glance into my rearview mirror and notice Braco and Dellatrix finally rolling over to their ride, waving away the frustrated ferry workers who throw their hands up in frustration.

"Why do you even need a car?" one of the bigfeet yells. "You're motorcycles!"

If I was anywhere else, I'm sure this encounter would've left me frustrated, but as the roar winds up into the lush green forest of the island, I can't help but let the sweet feelings of relaxation and relief wash over me. Everything here is quiet and calm, untouched in a way that is honestly quite inspiring.

Back in the city, I found myself frustrated by the repetition of it all, but out here it feels like nothing has even started happening yet. Gazing out at the thick tree trunks that whip past, I find my mind drifting back hundreds of years to when they were just saplings, wondering how little has actually changed. Sure, this road probably didn't exist back then, but just a few yards off the cement these plants have likely gone completely undisturbed.

Minerma's cabin is on the far end of the island, in a location even more desolate than this one, but on the way there I pass through a small town with a selection of quaint little stores and restaurants. Most of them are closed down for the season, but a few remain open to serve the locals.

Having stopped before the ferry ride, I'm fully stocked with groceries and supplies, so I continue on my way.

Honestly, all I want to do is get to the cabin and start spellcrafting, a desire that I haven't felt in a long, long time. I have no idea what's going to come out when I sit down, no mystical instructions or goals yet mapped out in my head. For all I know it could all be complete trash.

The important thing, however, is that I actually *want* to create magic again. This gorgeous landscape around me is just too good to let go of, the scent of the pines and the soft cool touch of the afternoon fog against my skin as I roll the windows down. I need to capture this.

The road winds more and more as I go, twisting and turning through the woods until, eventually, the pavement gives way to crunching gravel. I slow down to a crawl, glancing around for any sign of an address.

Soon enough, the trees open up to a glorious view of the ocean. I'm atop a hill and looking down at a grassy runway that leads to the water, three or four small cabins lining the road.

The top cabin has a number nailed to the side, spelled out in selection of twisted, tan driftwood.

"Seven twenty-two, Gorb Road," I say aloud to myself. This is the place.

I pull down the dirt road and then veer off to the side, parking behind my new cabin so as not to block the beautiful ocean view from within. From here, I can see that there's a vaguely maintained community dock on the beach below, a single, large yacht tied up to it but floating empty in the soft afternoon waves.

I climb out of my car and head up to the cabin, pulling out a key that Minerma gave to me back in New York. I use it to open the cabin door.

The second that I step inside this place, I'm utterly blown away by its quiet, unassuming charm. There's a fireplace against the back wall with a framed map of the island above it. Two massive couches sit before this, facing one another with a coffee table in between. The furniture is overstuffed and slightly too big for the space, by that only adds to its cozy charm. In the other room is a kitchen and out front is a deck with a perfect view of the grassy hill and the beach below.

The deck, of course, would be a perfect place to spend my days spellcrafting, but for now it's a little cold out. Off to my left is a small bedroom, but it's too dark and there's not much of a view, so I finally decide that the large fluffy couches are my best bet, something that I certainly can't complain about.

I spend the next half an hour loading in my bags and groceries, carrying them into the kitchen and fully stocking the fridge for the days ahead.

Finally, when all of this is finished, I make some tea and then pull my laptop from its case, carefully bringing them both over to the couch. I set my supplies out before me, the perfect spellcrafting kit complete with various sample components and a bit of scratch parchment, then take a deep breath, excited to finally begin the next stage of my career.

Of course, there's still one ingredient left, and although it doesn't need to be here for the crafting of this new spell, it's important to have around symbolically.

I reach into my bag and pull out my wand, setting it on the table before me.

Wizards need their wands to cast spells, unlike bards who can simply sing or perform on a musical instrument to create magical effects, or warlocks who can manifest their magical powers through a pact with some omnipresent author named Chuck.

Sometimes I'm jealous of these other spellcasters who don't require a wand, but then I remember the immutable fact that wizards are still the most powerful of them all.

Now, I'm ready.

I raise my fingers, but before they can touch down on the keyboard there's a loud, thunderous thump that rattles through the walls, shaking every dish in the nearby cupboard.

I sit up straight, not quite sure what's happening. Immediately, my mind begins to question whether or not there are trolls here on Portork Island, but seconds later another loud thump rattles through the cabin, and then another and another, creating a steady rhythm. Although there's no melody present, it quickly becomes apparent that whatever is making this racket is not a natural occurrence.

I stand up and walk over to the deck, throwing open my door as I'm immediately hit with even more of the earsplitting sound. The tones are no longer muffled, and it now becomes apparent that the noise is the heavy beat of a large rock and roll drum kit.

Of course, it's much too loud to be just any old drum set. Whatever this is has been amplified and projected through speakers, rumbling across this beachfront cove at a near supernatural volume.

I glance down at one of the cabins below and gasp in shock at what I see. When I'd arrived earlier, these buildings showed no signs of life, but now Dellatrix and Braco's sports car has been parked right next to one of them, the curtains of the small building drawn, but every light on within.

After holding my tongue back on the ferry, I find myself completely out of restraint.

Boiling over with rage and frustration, I march down off of the deck and head towards this outrageous cacophony, the rhythmic sounds growing louder and louder with every step. Soon enough, I've completely traversed the grassy hill, arriving at the cabin's front door and knocking loudly.

Unfortunately, the drums are hammering away so loud that there's no way for the knocks of my small hand to be heard. Going full Brooklyn, I take another approach, kicking my foot against the door as hard as I can. I can see the wooden frame shake, but the sound is still not quite loud enough to draw the attention of anyone inside.

Suddenly, the drums stop, if only for a moment. Seeing my opportunity, I give the door one more kick as hard as I can.

"Get out here!" I scream at the top of my lungs. "I need to have a word."

There's a brief moment of silence from behind the door, and then seconds later a muffled eruption of that same obnoxious laugher I'd heard back on the ferry. Eventually, the laugher quiets down into a soft giggle and then disappears completely, replaced instead by some quick chatter that I can't quite discern.

"I'm not going away," I call out. "Not until you come out here!"

The only thing I receive in return is utter silence from inside.

I raise my hand to pound on the door one last time when suddenly it opens wide and I stop dead in my tracks. I'd fully expected to find the motorcycles standing before me, with those same obnoxious grins, but what I receive could not be any farther removed.

There in the doorway is a tall, breathtakingly handsome dinosaur, shirtless and chiseled in all of his muscular glory. He's covered in tattoos, giving his scaly green canvas an even more exotic edge, and his eyes are wide and yellow. His face is covered in a perfectly timed five o' clock shadow, not long enough to be a beard, but nicely emphasizing his dark features and strong jaw. His hair is long and dark, providing an angsty, gothic frame to his handsome mug.

He appears to be a parasaurolophus.

"Hi," is all that I can manage to say, the word falling limply from my mouth.

"I'm Snabe," the prehistoric creature says in a thick, British accent, "and you must be Marriet."

"Harriet," I correct him, stumbling over the word a bit.

"Right. The bikes said they met you on the boat, huh?" Snabe continues.

I'm vaguely aware that I'm supposed to respond at this point, but I'm just too entranced by Snabe's shirtless body to say anything. The dinosaur is damn near comically toned, his rugged prehistoric shape something that shouldn't naturally exist outside of the pages of fitness magazines or a romance book cover.

I've seen plenty of handsome dinosaurs before and still managed to maintain a coherent conversation, but something about Snabe twists my brain completely around on itself, rendering me helpless.

I feel like I've seen him somewhere before.

"You alright?" the parasaurolophus asks with a laugh, breaking through my mental haze once more and pulling me back to reality.

"I'm sorry," I stammer, shaking my head from side to side as though it might clear out the cobwebs within.

"I asked if you were alright," Snabe repeats. "That's not really an answer."

"Yeah, I just lost my train of thought there for a minute," I confess.

"Understandable," Snabe retorts with a smirk.

The second that he says this I find myself completely disengaged from the parasaurolophus's charms. He's implying, of course, that he's well aware of just how attractive he is, which couldn't be more off putting. He's not wrong, but a little humility would go a long way.

"You're making a lot of noise," I finally inform Snabe. "What are you doing in there?"

"Writing drum parts for a songspell I'm working on," he explains, very matter-of-factly. "We've got a whole studio set up in here, would you like to come in and listen?"

Ugh. Suddenly, it all makes sense. He may be a fellow spellcrafter, but he's also a bard. Bards, as I mentioned before, are those who manifest magical effects through musical means, rather than the written word of spell books.

Snabe's eyes make their way up and down my body, checking me out.

"I'm sorry," he suddenly blurts, noticing my appalled expression. "I'm just written this way."

"What?" I question, confused.

"It's a trope in romance," the dinosaur continues to explain. "The more of an asshole I am in this part of the book, the better the payoff is when you change me later on."

"I have no idea what you're talking about," I reply, shaking my head from side to side.

"It's okay," the parasaurolophus continues. "Just as long as it's clear this is *fiction*. In the real world you should probably just break up with someone who acts like this, or even quit their class."

I force the flicker of attraction out of my head immediately. I'm better than this, and as far as I can tell, Snabe is a complete asshole that makes very little sense.

Still, his dinosaur face remains strikingly familiar.

Suddenly, it clicks.

"Oh my god," I blurt. "Are you Snabe Rezmor? The bard from Seven Inch Nails?"

"When we're recording, I'm the whole band, actually," he confirms. "Singer, guitarist… today I'm the drummer."

Now the fight to quell my attraction is even more difficult. It takes everything I can to push the feelings of arousal out of my mind, locking them deep down in the basement and throwing away the key.

Seven Inch Nails was one of my favorite bardic troupes back in wizarding college. Thundering industrial rhythms, incredible musicianship and heart wrenching vocals were their trademarks, a dark metamagic group that hit all the marks yet somehow still managed to bring something entirely new to the bardic spell scene. They were critical darlings for a while, putting out at least three hit spell collections that I was aware of. Eventually, my interest faded.

Still, any time one of their songspells comes on the radio, I can't help but turn it up.

"I don't love bardic spells, or metamagic… but I'm a huge fan," I admit.

"The feelings mutual, darling," Snabe replies in his thick accent, offering me a playful wink.

Once more, I'm equal parts disgusted and intrigued.

"Listen, can you just keep it down in there? I'm on the island for some peace and quiet," I explain. "The volume in your studio is up so loud that it's literally shaking my house."

"Drums are loud," Snabe informs me, something that I clearly knew already.

"Yes, but you're amplifying them to be even louder," I continue.

"So you want me to turn it down?" Snabe clarifies again.

"That would be wonderful," I inform him. "Please."

The rockstar bard considers this for a moment, then shakes his head. "No."

I'm completely floored by his response, not quite sure if I heard him correctly despite the fact that his reply was a single word, loud and clear. Snabe's rude defiance has flown in the face of any normal social interaction, and that says a lot coming from a New Yorker. Even if he refuses to change the volume, he's at least supposed to lie about it while we're standing face to face.

"So you're just... not gonna turn it down?" I question, utterly dumbfounded.

"Nope," the dinosaur confirms, shaking his head from side to side. "I need to know if the beat's any good before we start writing to it, and I won't be able to tell unless it's really slamming. You came out to this island for a place to be quiet, I came out here to be loud."

Snabe opens his arms wide, gesturing across the hillside and towards the trees beyond, while simultaneously showing off his incredible biceps. "See, nobody's here to care about the noise. Until you showed up, of course."

I let out a long sigh. "Can't we reach a compromise?"

"Afraid not," the parasaurolophus bard replies flatly. "Not yet anyway. This is still the part of the story where I'm a huge asshole."

"Why do you keep saying that?" I blurt. "What story?"

"I'm a metamagic bard, remember?" the handsome dinosaur clarifies. "I create magical spells that draw on a meta awareness of The Tingleverse."

"So?" I continue.

"*So* I'm well aware this is a bad boy romance novel, and I've got a job to do," he explains. "Trust me, I don't love acting this way, either. I guess it's just important to remember just because a fictional character is a jerk, it doesn't mean the author is, too. Likewise, if a fictional character is sweet and awesome, their author could still be really awful and bigoted."

"Why are you telling me this?" I question.

"I'm not telling you, I'm telling the reader," the dinosaur informs me.

Suddenly, from out of the darkness behind Snabe rolls the familiar form of Dellatrix, swaying her tires from side to side with a sensual grace that is both annoying and impressive. The sentient motorcycle is wearing an oversized, ripped tee shirt with the logo of a heavy metal band emblazoned across the front, too twisted to read and likely borrowed from Snabe. She carries a half empty bottle of chocolate milk in her hand.

"Check out her shoes," Dellatrix says to Snabe, teasingly.

Snabe glances down at the same ratty slip-ons that I've been wearing all day.

"Uh, yeah," the dinosaur bard offers, clearly not understanding how he's supposed to react.

"Cute, right?" Dellatrix continues, laying on the sarcasm on as thick as she can.

"Yeah, they're pretty cool," Snabe finally replies.

Frustrated, Dellatrix steps between us and pulls the cabin door closed. "Bye sweetie, he's got work to do."

The wooden door slams shut, leaving me standing in silence and confusion. I'm still completely blown away by the events that just transpired.

For a few seconds, there's utter peace and calm in the air, the only sounds drifting across my ears those of the nearby birds and the soft waves rushing across the sand of the beach below.

It doesn't last however, and the next thing I know, the thunderous, thumping crashes begin again.

I consider knocking once more, but quickly remind myself that Snabe has already been very clear about his intentions of listening to me. There will be no compromise.

Now there's only one option left, and although there's a deep dark part of me that would love to remain cool in the eyes of this breathtakingly handsome parasaurolophus spellsmith, the logical portion of my mind knows exactly what needs to be done.

I turn and march back up to my cabin, grabbing ahold of the phone and dialing the island sheriff.

SLASHED

3

It doesn't take long for the sheriff to arrive, especially considering the size of Portork Island and just how far out of town we are, but when I factor in how little they probably have on their plate out here, it all starts to make sense.

I'm watching from the windows of my cabin, peering up over the sill as I stare down the hill towards Snabe's place.

The sheriff, a handsome purple unicorn, pulls right up next to the bright yellow sports car, climbing out of his ride and then taking in this exotic vehicle as though it's some strange craft from another planet. Eventually, he makes his way over to Snabe's cabin door, but thanks to the crashing drums that have been emanating non-stop from within since I left, the sheriff ends up having the exact same problem that I did. Nobody can hear him knocking.

Eventually, the unicorn ends up taking a stroll around the house, finally catching someone's attention through a nearby window. He returns back to the front door, which opens to reveal Snabe once more in all of his shirtless, tatted up glory.

"Why does he have to be such an asshole?" I find myself mumbling aloud.

I watch as the two men talk, their faces slowly going from stern to good-natured.

"No, no, no!" I stammer to myself, watching as the dinosaur and unicorn begin to joke with one another, laughing together at some mysterious punch line.

To my dismay, Snabe suddenly opens up his mouth and begins to sing, the magical incantation short and to the point. I can see waves of bardic energy emitting from his throat in sizzling vapors, washing across the unicorn sheriff's face. Soon enough, the unicorn is nodding along with the parasaurolophus in a fit of feverish enthusiasm.

Suddenly, Snabe points up towards my window, offering a wave and abruptly causing me to duck out of sight.

When I finally muster up the courage to peek back over the sill, both of the creatures are gone, but the sheriff's patrol car is still parked out front. Seconds later, there's a loud, authoritative knock at my door.

I walk over, opening it up to find the unicorn sheriff standing before me. He's got a wide brimmed hat and silver hair that pushes out from under it ever so slightly, as well as a large, brilliant white moustache. The unicorn's horn pops out through a hole in the middle of his hat, twinkling under the light. The guy looks like everything a big city girl like me would imagine in a lawman from these parts.

"Harriet Porber?" he questions.

I nod. "That's me. I'm the one who called."

"You're new around here, right?" the unicorn continues.

"That's right," I reply with a nod.

The unicorn laughs. "Well, as long as you're not here to drink my blood, you'll fit in just fine around here. I'm Sheriff Thomson. Snabe's gonna quiet down over there now," the unicorn assures me. "I gave him a warning and told him to take a break for the day, but most days he's allowed to make noise from noon until sundown. Maybe not *so* damn loud, though. If he pumps the volume up like that again, you just give me a call, alright?"

I smile, thankful for this resolution that appears to be the basic comprise I'd asked for in the first place.

"Thank you, Sheriff," I offer with a smile.

"Have a good rest of your day, ma'am," he tells me, tilting his hat before turning around and heading back down towards his car.

Now that things have settled a bit, I immediately turn my attention back to the task at hand, the entire reason that I took this transatlantic trip in the first place. I collapse into the big comfy sofa and set my laptop on my knees, opening up a new document and staring down at the beautiful white page before me. There's something absolutely majestic about its perfectly blank surface, an endless field of empty pixels just waiting for me to dance my clever incantations across it.

Of course, there's also something quite intimidating about this. What if I start writing this spell and end up hating every magical sequence? What if this entire trip has been for nothing, and I'm just as uninspired as I was back home?

When I first arrived here at the cabin, there was the spark of something powerful dancing around within me, I was excited to write and express myself, thrilled just to be sitting here with my word processor and a cup of tea.

Now, the anxiety is sneaking back.

I recognize almost immediately that nothing is gonna get done with this kind of mind frame. My interactions with Snabe, Dellatrix and Braco have been less than pleasant, and that feeling has started to erode away at whatever magical inspiration I'd been building up over the course of today's travel.

On top of that, I haven't even had lunch yet.

I glance at the nearby wall clock, a hanging wooden piece that looks as though it was salvaged from the cabin of some ancient pirate ship. It's already two in the afternoon, well past my typical noon meal and probably adding to the subtle discomfort that's been making its way through every aspect of my thoughts.

I consider cracking open some of the food that I'd brought to the island, but instead quickly realize that if I'm actually gonna reboot my brain, I need to leave the house for a while. A nice late lunch back in town might be exactly what I need to cool off.

Without hesitation, I grab my coat and head for the door, hopeful that this little trip will turn things around for me.

Arriving back in town, I find myself with few food options to choose from, which is actually kind of nice. In Brooklyn, there's a different kind of cuisine on every corner, with so much variety that it can often be overwhelming. Sometimes, the most frustrating part about eating out is deciding where to go while you stand around getting hungrier and hungry.

I stare up at the two signs before me. To my left is Captain Orion's Cove, and to my right is the Hugo Café; the only two places serving food over the off-season, apparently.

Excited to try out some of the local English seafood, I make my way towards Captain Orion's Cove, heading down a small alley between two buildings and eventually finding myself at a tan, nondescript doorway. I push through.

Almost immediately, my senses are overwhelmed by warmth and flavor, the scent of sizzling fish wafting over me in the most glorious of ways.

Back home, a place like this would find grease floating through the air, creating a sickening film across your skin that only got thicker the longer you hung around for. Instead, I'm treated to a pleasant freshness, with bountiful spices mulled into a delicious seafood aroma.

"Have a seat anywhere," an older woman calls over.

The view from this restaurant is incredible, with floor to ceiling windows that stretch from one end of the room to the other and put the cove before us on glorious display. I take a seat in the corner so that I can see everything, my eyes lingering on the coastline as it snakes off in the distance.

"You're new around here," the waitress offers, dropping off a menu and bringing me a tall glass of water.

"Just arrived this morning," I inform her.

"Oh yeah? Where from?" the woman continues, making pleasant conversation.

I can tell from her demeanor that my waitress is genuinely interested in what I have to say, something that I'm not at all used to. She's got a strange look about her; small, with rather large ears that almost appear to be pointed at the end.

"New York," I offer. "Brooklyn."

The waitress nods. "Ah. There's been a lot of you big city folks stopping by lately. We've got a new parasaurolophus regular from Bristol."

My breath catches in my throat. I consider whether or not I should say anything or hold my tongue, not wanting to bring any negativity into this sweet woman's perfectly joyful existence.

Unfortunately, I just can't help myself.

"We've met," I finally say, practically spitting the words out. "He's a dick."

The waitress chuckles and nods. "Sounds about right. Not a lot of folks around here care for the guy."

"And you?" I continue.

The woman considers my question for a moment, apparently weighing several different responses in her head. "He's pretty rough around the edges," she finally offers, "and I certainly don't like the ladies he brings around."

Suddenly, the waitress stops herself.

"I mean, not all of them," she clarifies gently.

I shake my head. "I'm not one of his… girlfriends. Don't worry."

"Well, alright," the waitress confirms with a nod. "Either way, he's actually a very sweet dinosaur when you get to know him. Tips very well."

"I find that hard to believe," I blurt, losing control of my internal filter completely. "That asshole doesn't have a giving bone in his body."

The waitress smiles but says nothing in return. It takes a moment, but eventually her expression begins to crack, faltering under the pressure of some great internal weight. It suddenly looks as though she's about to cry.

"He gives quite a bit, actually," the woman informs me, trying to keep it together. "He always tipped well, but when he found out my daughter was sick…" the woman trails off, then finally collects herself. "He tips very well."

"I'm sorry," I stammer, completely taken off guard by this unexpected show of emotion. The story itself is surprising, too. It's hard to believe that we're actually talking about the same person.

Immediately, the woman switches back into her happy and helpful waitress mode, wiping away a tear and then waving off my concerns. "It's fine, it's fine," she assures me. "What can I get you to eat?"

"How about the cod spaghetti?" I suggest.

"Good choice," the woman replies, taking my menu back and then heading off towards the kitchen to put in my order.

I stare out the window again, trying to picture the self-righteous asshole I'd encountered earlier actually going out of his way for someone else. As a wizard who regularly flirts with the limits of the physical realm, I'm well aware that none of us are actually the one-dimension cutouts we sometimes appear to be at first glance, but it's still hard come to terms with the divide between Snabe's deeply flawed character traits and his apparent incredible generosity.

Of course, whatever amount of money he's given to the waitress is probably just pocket change to him, I remind myself. Seven Inch Nails had some massive bardic spells, still getting spins on the radio and popping up in commercials to this day. As I recall, he was once a highly regarded magic teacher, as well, and might even be collecting money from the spells he crafted back in magic school for the Lizardin frat.

That metamagic really sells.

Eventually, my meal arrives and I spend the next hour or so taking bites while staring out at the incredible scenery before me. I'm in no rush, intentionally hoping to slow my life down to a crawl. I want to savor this, allowing my body a chance to fully process the events of the day.

The whole time I consume my lunch, not a single other patron comes in the visit the restaurant.

When I finally finish, I stand and thank my waitress for my incredible meal. I tip her generously, not quite as much as Snabe, I'm sure, but enough for her to know that I care.

Heading out to the car, I'm simmering with excitement once more, ready to head home and hit the keyboard running. Unfortunately, this feeling doesn't last long.

The second I see my car a startled gasp erupts from my lips. I can't believe what I'm looking at, shocked that someone would actually take things this far.

The vehicle is sitting noticeably lower to the ground, all four of its tires completely slashed open and deflated into puddles of grey rubber.

"What the fuck," I stammer, my knees nearly giving out below me. I grab onto the nearby wall to steady myself, struggling to catch my breath.

After taking a moment to calm down, I slowly walk around the entire perimeter of my vehicle to observe the damage.

Without my wand, which unfortunately sits on my desk back at the cabin, the tires are irrepairable, completely shredded in some spots and well beyond any kind of patch. I have a single spare in the trunk, but that's not going to do me any good. Thankfully, I paid for insurance on the rental, but who knows how long a fix is going to take.

Even more importantly, is there a working auto mechanic on the island?

Not knowing where else to turn, I head back into the restaurant, immediately greeted by my waitress once more.

"Did you forget something?" the woman questions.

I shake my head, trying to remain as calm as possible. "Is there are place that can repair tires around here?" I ask. "Four of them."

"All four tires?" the woman repeats back in confused alarm. "What did you run over?"

I shake my head. "Nothing, I can think of something that I *should've* run over, though."

"There's one auto shop on the island," the waitress explains. "Orabello runs it, but he's on the mainland today. Won't be back until tomorrow morning."

I let out a long sigh. "Any taxis around here?"

The woman shakes her head. "I'm sorry."

Not being one to just let life run me over without putting up a fight, I immediately spring into action. "Now, I'm guessing that if I call this auto shop it's gonna take me straight to voicemail, correct?" I question.

The waitress nods. "Nobody's there."

"Can you call Orabello's personal number and have him repair my tires first thing in the morning?" I ask. "I've got insurance, he can charge whatever he wants."

The woman nods, then strolls over to the nearby hostess counter and grabs a pen and a paper. "Just write down your address and I'll have him drive it over to you after he's finished."

I do as I'm told, jotting down my information before handing the paper back and then thanking the waitress for her help. Once finished, I turn around and start heading back towards the door of the restaurant.

"Where are you headed now?" the woman calls out from behind me.

"I'm walking home," I inform her.

The second I begin my trek my mind goes into lockdown, completely blocking out just how cold it is and how many miles I'll have to go. I don't think about the fact that by the time I get home the sun will be setting and I'll probably have to head right to bed in severe exhaustion. I also don't think about the fact that I'm going to get very, very thirsty and have no idea if there's any place to stop for drinkable water along the way.

Instead, I give myself permission to start imagining things, to let the seeds of a spell start to bloom within my mind. I'm here to break out of my monotonous routine, and this certainly fits the bill.

For the first time in quite a while, I can actually feel the incantations bubbling up within me. This morning I was feeling inspired to spellcraft, but the writing itself lacked focus. Now, however, I'm getting a sense of what I want this spell to be.

What if there was a spell that could literally bend the hands of fate? A catch all ritual that would provide you with the thing you needed most before you even knew you needed it? I could've cast it before I left the house this evening, then later discovered that my wand had somehow fallen into my bag.

The tires would be repaired and I'd be well on my way.

Of course, this is a crazy thought. A spell this broad has never been attempted and would likely never work, but the inspiration feels incredible.

A few cars pass me by as I'm walking down the road, and I make halfhearted attempts to hitchhike that go entirely ignored.

About two hours into my walk, however, one of the cars slows down.

"Where you headed?" calls the familiar motorcycle voice of Dellatrix from her yellow sports car. "You shouldn't be out here walking in those fancy, expensive shoes."

"Yeah, they're too cute," Braco yells, piling it on.

I stop dead in my tracks, nearly boiling over in anger. I have no evidence that either of these girls, nor Snabe himself, had anything to do with my tire slashing, but there aren't many other people on the island, and certainly none that I've got a conflict with.

I turn towards the car and open my mouth, ready to launch into a scathing diatribe, but before the words have a chance to tumble out, Dellatrix hits the gas hard. The next thing I know, the motorcycles are rocketing off down the road, their roaring engine drowning out the sound of my shouts as they disappear around the corner and off into the distance.

Soon enough, the only thing left of them is the thunderous sound of their motor echoing fainting through the trees, getting quieter and quieter with every passing second. Eventually, it fades completely, leaving me with nothing more than my own thoughts and the soft sound of the breeze through the trees above.

During the rest of my walk, any creative clarity has been completely dismantled. Instead, all that I can focus on now is my seething frustration.

The trek is so long that, by the time I arrive back at my cabin, I've calmed down enough to decline marching right up to that stupid yellow car and busting out every window. I'm tempted though; very, very tempted.

Instead, I head to my front door and start digging through my coat pocket in search of the key, but stop when I hear something faintly drifting up from the beach. It's music; soft, pleasant music.

If I'm to be perfectly honest, a little acoustic guitar during a sunset as beautiful as this one would usually be cause for celebration, but at this point I'm just too frazzled to handle it.

The sheriff said no more music today, and the first thing I hear when arriving back home for the night is even more music.

This is just too much to handle.

I allow myself to go full New Yorker.

The next thing I know, I'm marching down the grassy hill towards the water below, a powerful confidence in my step that seems almost superhuman. It's as though I'm hovering above myself, watching the scene unfold from somewhere outside my own body. I've completely given up the reins that once held me back, dismissing any sense of mercy for these forces that continue to assault my senses.

I reach the bottom of the hill, finding a quaint set of cement stairs the leads down to the beach and directly connects to the dock. Beyond, this wooden structure stretches out into the deep blue water, an incredible sight as the sun begins its decent below the horizon line. In any other situation, I'd stop to take it all in, but at this point I've got other things on my mind; mainly, the silhouetted parasaurolophus bard sitting peacefully at the end of the dock while he strums his guitar, gazing off into the sunset. I can tell he's working on a songspell, because vapors of magical energy are wafting peacefully across the surface of the water, struggling to find their form but not quite there yet.

Snabe's attention is so consumed by the incredible wash of oranges and purples painting the sky before him, that he doesn't even seem to notice me approaching from the rear.

He *does* notice, however, when I silently grab the guitar from his hands, and with one powerful toss, throw it as far as I can out into the water. The instrument lands with a splash, floating for a moment and then slowly filling with water until it begins its gradual decent towards the ocean floor.

The dinosaur stands up without a word and turns to face me, still completely shirtless despite the cold chill in the air. We stare at one another in silence for a good while, taking each other in.

"That was a really expensive guitar," Snabe finally says, flatly.

"I'm sure you can afford a new one," I remind him.

The frustratingly attractive prehistoric creature thinks about this for a moment. "You're right," he finally tells me, then strolls past on the narrow dock, nearly knocking me out of the way.

"Hey! Where are you going?" I question.

Snabe doesn't answer, but turns when he arrives at his massive boat and then climbs aboard. I follow closely behind, losing track of the bard for a moment until he suddenly emerges from the cabin with yet another beautifully crafted acoustic guitar.

The muscular dinosaur walks over and takes a seat in one of the many white leather couches that line the back of the boat, quickly picking up right where he left off. He begins to strum softly, turning to gaze out across the ocean at the fading sun.

"You promised there would be no more music today," I remind him.

"No more *loud* music," Snabe clarifies.

"That's not what I heard," I counter.

Snabe shrugs. "That's what I told Sheriff Thomson," he informs me. "You can call him if you'd like."

I stand in silence, suddenly feeling utterly defeated. Snabe's song continues to dance across the water, echoing back towards us from every direction around the cove. To be honest, it's a beautiful piece of music, and now that my anger has subsided a bit I can finally admit this to myself.

"You like it?" Snabe asks, apparently picking up on something.

I nod.

Snabe smiles and then stands up, strolling over to the boat's steering wheel and control panel. I can't help watching the parasaurolophus's powerful muscles pulse as he moves.

Snabe reaches the controls and casually presses a button. "Better record it then," he tells me.

The musician strolls back over and takes his seat once more, starting in with his acoustic strums from the very beginning of the arrangement.

"What was that all about?" I finally ask, my curiosity getting the best of me.

"What was what?" Snabe questions, stopping for a moment.

"You just pressed that button," I remind him.

Snabe laughs. "Oh yeah. That's to start recording. I rigged up the back of the boat with microphones, that way if I'm out on the water when I get inspired to craft a songspell, I can just press a button and jot the idea down. There's no phone service on the water, so it all gets sent back up to the cabin through satellites."

"Why not just use a handheld recorder like normal people?" I question. "Or just record it on your phone and then send it to yourself when you get back?"

Snabe considers this and then shrugs. "Don't know. My way just seemed cooler," he offers through a thick British drawl. "It's got Bluetooth, too. Can I see your phone?"

I shake my head.

"Okay, just pull it out and connect then," he continues.

Reluctantly, I take my phone out of my pocket, immediately noticing the signal network emanating from Snabe's yacht.

"Password is *sherbet lime*," he says. "Play something."

I connect with no problem and then press play on the first song in my library I can think of, a soft indie folk track that aligns with the beautiful sunset above us.

Suddenly, earsplitting sound erupts from the boat, so loud that it nearly knocks me over backwards. I immediately fumble with my phone, struggling to turn it off as the heavy vibration of bass reverberates through my body.

Finally, I press the stop button, plunging us back into peaceful silence as the overwhelming wave of sound continues to echo out across the water, eventually disappearing in the distance.

"Nice, right?" Snabe questions.

"It's a little loud," I inform him.

The dinosaur bard shrugs.

My eyes wander across the gorgeous yacht. "Just how rich are you?" I finally ask.

"Pretty rich," Snabe informs me. "I didn't really earn it, though. I was written into incredible wealth by Chuck Tingle, the author. You can't really just be a bad boy in books like this, you've gotta be a *billionaire* bad boy. It's kinda toxic, actually."

I take a deep breath. "You know, not all of us are wealthy enough to just buy a full set of new tires. You're lucky that was a rental and I've got insurance."

Snabe narrows his eyes. "I have no idea what you're talking about."

"Ask Dellatrix," I retort.

Suddenly, the hulking dinosaur's demeanor changes completely, consumed by a genuine concern. The shift is so drastic that I'd almost hard to believe, but it's also too blatant to ignore. "Are you alright? What happened?"

"Dellatrix and Braco slashed every tire on my car. I had to walk back from town," I inform him.

Snabe furrows his brow. "Are you sure it was them? Did you notice motorcycle tracks?"

I take a deep breath, frustrated by the question that I knew would eventually come. "No," I finally admit.

"Well, I'm sorry someone did that to you," Snabe continues. "I really am. I can talk to them anyway, just to see what I can find out. If they actually did that, then I'll send them packing."

The parasaurolophus is just too damn charming to hate, and in this moment I completely feel myself losing grip on my anger. The emotion is slipping away from me, no matter how desperately I struggle to maintain my connection to it.

"It's okay," I finally say. "I mean, it's not okay, but... I'll live. I'm sorry I threw your guitar in the water, but at least you've got another one."

"This one's not worth fifteen thousand dollars," Snabe replies with a chuckle, "but at least it works."

My heart skips a beat when I hear this, struggling to determine whether or not the bard is just messing with me. "Are you serious?" I finally ask.

Snabe nods. "Yeah, that one was from the sixties. I got it in an auction at the Bardic Spellcraft Hall Of Fame."

"Oh my god," I blurt. "I'm so, so sorry."

"Don't worry about it," the man offers, legitimately not upset.

"I wish I could repay you," I stammer. "I just... I don't have that kind of money."

"You could let me take you out on a date," Snabe retorts.

I'm completely taken off guard by this comment, and although my first instinct is to be excited by the prospect of a night out with this breathtakingly handsome British dinosaur, I'm also well aware of his type. Snabe may have his moments of sweetness, but he was a complete prick to me earlier in the day and I'm not quite ready to let go of that yet. This parasaurolophus is bad news any way you slice it, and I've got a spell to craft.

"No thanks," I tell him, then turn around without another word and start heading back up to the house.

Behind me, I can hear Snabe's haunting acoustic guitar song begin yet again, a beautiful piece of music that is somehow clawing its way out from the soul of this rugged and damaged dinosaur.

WHAT YOU NEED, WHEN YOU NEED IT

4

The loud buzz of my phone's vibration causes me to sit up in a state of frantic alarm, confused by the darkness around me. It takes a moment for me to get my bearings, struggling to remember where I am and how I got here. Back in New York, I rarely found myself in complete darkness, a bright neon sign or distant glowing skyline always creeping its way through my window, regardless of how thick my curtains were.

Fortunately, after a few frantic seconds, I remember the trials and tribulations of yesterday. I've travel to a land that is far removed from the horns and sirens that would normally greet my ears in the morning, a place where there is absolutely no manmade glow to be found.

Still, that doesn't explain why it's so damn dark out.

"Hello?" I groan, putting the phone to my ear.

"Harriet?" a familiar voice comes singing out from the other end of the line.

"Minerma?" I reply, still confused. "What time is it?"

"It's nine thirty, are you sleeping in?" my friend asks me. "I'm sorry, I should've waited. I know you had a long travel day and you're probably exhausted."

I let out a long sigh. "Well, yeah, I'm exhausted, but it's also three hours earlier here. The sun hasn't even come up yet."

"I'm so sorry," Minerma stammers. "I can call you back."

I sit up and rub my eyes, letting a long, satisfying stretch curl its way out across my body. "No, no, it's fine. I'm still on New York time anyway."

"Are you sure?" my agent questions.

"I'm fine," I assure her. "What's up?"

Minerma hesitates for a moment. "Well, I'm just calling to see how my favorite wizard's new spell is coming along. You have any moments of inspiration?"

I groan loudly, falling back into the thick ocean of blankets around me with a soft thud. "Minerma, it's only been a day. I need some time."

"I know, I know," my spellcraft agent assures me. "It's just, they're already breathing down my neck. They want to know what kind of direction you're headed in. Let's keep this one hot-to-trot."

"Direction takes time," I remind her. "You can't just force inspiration, that's why I'm here."

"I know, I'm sorry," Minerma sighs, then trails off a bit before changing the subject. "How's the cabin? I miss that place."

"It's beautiful, thank you so much for letting me stay here," I tell her. "I think this island is gonna bring something really incredible out of me."

"That's a good word to use!" Minerma blurts, excitedly. "*Incredible* spells are just what we're looking for."

I laugh. "I would imagine so. Now if the neighbors would just shut the hell up I could actually start writing it down."

"Neighbors?" Harriet questions. "That's a surprise. There's rarely anybody out there this time of year."

"There's a few assholes next door," I tell her. "Well, one asshole and his two motorcycles."

"Oh no," Minerma moans in recognition. "Snabe's there, isn't he?"

"You *know* him?" I blurt, sitting up again.

"I do," Minerma informs me, her voice sounding strangely defeated. "We grew up spending our summers on the island. Obviously, his family was much wealthier than mine, making the trip from Bristol and all, but they'd be out there for months at a time to make sure all that travel was worth it."

"Wow," I reply, trying to picture this arrogant prick as a humble little dinosaur, innocent and sweet. "Was he always this way?"

Minerma laughs. "Not at all. He was the most caring kid on the island. When the others would pick on me, he'd always have my back. We were best friends back then."

"That's not the dinosaur I met," I reply.

"You know, the two of you actually have a lot in common. He's a spellcrafter like you are, just in a different way. Plus, you're both trans," Minerma offers.

"Wait... really?" I blurt.

"You didn't know that?" Minerma continues, clearly a little shocked. "That's a huge part of his lyrics. He's trans and proud."

"Huh," is all that I can think to say in response. I never really paid attention to the words, I guess.

"Anyway, when the band was coming up he stopped taking trips to the island," Minerma continues. "In fact, I'm fairly certain the cabin was sold off to someone else. After Snabe hit it big with the Seven Inch Nails, he bought the place right back. By then, his whole personality had changed. It's like he was constantly trying to prove something to the rest of the world."

"He just went out and bought the same place back? That's... oddly sentimental," I reply.

"Well, it's Snabe in a nutshell," Minerma continues. "Sure he's a little rough around the edges, but there's a kind heart buried deep down in there somewhere."

"A *little* rough?" I scoff.

"Okay, very rough," Minerma replies. "Disastrous, even, but my point remains the same."

"He asked me on a date," I inform my friend.

My agent laughs. "Are you gonna go?"

I'm utterly shocked to hear this question coming from my otherwise strait-laced friend. Minerma is not much of a risk taker, so that fact that she would even consider this says a lot about her true feelings regarding Snabe. She obviously still sees the dinosaur as that innocent kid who would go far out of his way to protect her.

A chill of creeping arousal immediately runs down the length of my spine.

"I don't know," I finally admit. "I wasn't gonna go, but now for some reason I'm not so sure."

"Normally, I wouldn't say this, but desperate times call for desperate measures," Minerma states bluntly. "If you're looking for inspiration, I don't see how a date with that silly bard could hurt. Honestly, you're the only woman I'd trust to handle him, and like I said, you've probably got more in common than you'd think. Talk spellcraft!"

"I'll consider it," I tell my agent, then take a deep breath, stretching out across the bed and yawning loudly. "I've gotta go," I inform her. "Feeling inspired."

"Thank god," Minerma replies. "Call when you've got something."

I hang up and climb to my feet, scratching the wild mess of hair atop my head as I stumble out into the living room. The sun has just barely started to rise, casting the picturesque scene before me with long, orange shadows.

Today is the first day of the rest of my life, I remind myself. I feel confident that I'll be able to get a few words down this afternoon, even if it's just some rough outlines of the ideas that have been floating through my head. Honestly, anything would be fantastic. All I need is the slightest hint of forward progress, a tiny little nod from the universe that this trip has been for a reason.

I quickly get to work brewing up my morning chocolate milk and fixing myself a bowl of spaghetti, then bring them both over to the couch where my laptop is waiting.

This is it.

Suddenly, there's a series of three loud knocks against the back door. I sit up straight, incredibly curious about who could be calling at such an early hour, especially out here in a place like this.

"Hello?" I yell out.

Three more knocks rattle out across my ears, continuing to shatter the silence of the morning.

I stand up and walk over to the door, peeking out through the eyehole to see Dellatrix standing there awkwardly, shifting her weight on and off her kickstand. She looks disheveled and messy, her dark makeup slightly runny beneath her eyes.

"What do you want?" I call through the door, not trusting this sentient motorbike for a second.

"To talk," Dellatrix retorts bluntly.

"This early in the morning?" I reply.

"Don't you mean this late at night?" Dellatrix counter, then laughs loudly to herself.

I now notice that the motorcycle is utterly drunk off of her ass. I have no doubt she's telling the truth, and that Dellatrix has been up all night, tossing back chocolate milk from dusk until dawn.

"Just open the fucking door!" the dark motorbike suddenly yells, slamming the nearby frame with her fist so hard that it causes me to jump in surprise.

"You should go home," I tell her sternly.

"*I* should go home?" the woman laughs, clearly offended by this suggestion. "I was here way before you showed up, sweetie. I've been with Snabe for two years, and it was going just fine until you came by with your shitty shoes and your *bad hair.*"

I furrow my brow.

"Okay, well… I don't know what to tell you," I call back through the door.

"Tell me you'll stop talking to Snabe," Dellatrix groans.

I hesitate. This would've been much easier to do if she'd come by just hours earlier, but after my conversation with Minerma, I'm beginning to realize that there might actually be something worth saving behind the dinosaur's obnoxious, bad boy façade. Still, at this point I'll do anything to get her off of my porch.

Finally, I throw open the door in frustration, staring down Dellatrix face to face.

"You look like shit," the motorcycle tells me, but I ignore her.

"Why would I want to talk to that asshole?" I question. "Snabe is one of the rudest dinosaurs I've ever met in my life, and I'm from New York."

Dellatrix smirks, struggling to hide her expression but unable to keep it from creeping its way out across her face. "I know that he asked you on a date," Dellatrix finally informs me.

I say nothing in return, remaining tight lipped before this motorcycle who stares daggers into me. She's been quite belligerent this whole time, but now her demeanor shifts into a focused intensity. There's something dangerous behind her eyes, something I'd be remiss to ignore.

"Are you gonna go out with him?" Dellatrix continues.

"I don't know," I finally admit, not wanting to start a fight, but loving the fact that I have something to hold over this awful machine's head.

Dellatrix can barely hold herself together as the intensity within continues to boil, refusing to let loose as it pushes even harder against the edge of her civility.

At this point, however, my wizard's curiosity takes hold. I've always had a passion for interesting characters, and when I see someone as fanatical as Dellatrix, it's impossible for me to ignore. I want to know what brought her to this place of desperation, for better or worse.

"I'm confused," I finally admit. "Isn't Braco dating Snabe, too."

Dellatrix scoffs. "They're not *dating*."

"Then what *are* they doing?" I continue.

"That's a situation for me to take care of," Dellatrix informs me sternly. "I'm calling the shots. Nobody else."

"What about Snabe?" I push.

"*I* call the shots," Dellatrix repeats.

I consider her words for a moment. "I think I'm gonna take him up on that date," I finally say, then close the door in her face.

I stare back out through the peephole for a moment, watching as Dellatrix stands before my door in complete shock. She's frozen in place, her mind racing but her body still. That rage behind her eyes continues to lurk, flickering even more brilliant than ever, but even now it refuses to overflow completely.

Eventually, Dellatrix turns around and begins to roll away, stopping suddenly when she sees a large rock on the ground. I watch as the motorcycle tilts down to pick it up, turning over the hard surface in her hand as she inspects every imperfection. Dellatrix begins to glance back and forth between the rock and my bedroom window, clearly considering a number of options.

I'm just about to throw open to door once more and give her a piece of my mind, but seconds later the stone falls from Dellatrix's hand, thumping softly onto the dewy morning grass.

Dellatrix wobbles away, back down towards her cabin.

Feeling strangely renewed by this moment of emotional intensity, I stroll over to the kitchen table and sit down, opening up my laptop. So far, the couch hasn't been going too well, so now I'm trying out a place that's slightly less comfortable, hoping the workflow will kick into gear.

Dellatrix is a terrible person, that's for sure, but there's something about her that fascinates me. Her dedication to Snabe goes way beyond any healthy relationship, and it makes me wonder how far she would actually take things.

Suddenly, my fingers begin to fly across the keyboard below, rows and rows of frantic incantation slowly filling the screen. It's as though the floodgates of magical inspiration have been busted open.

I spend the next few hours here at my laptop, typing away as the shadows outside begin to shrink, the orange morning sky transforming into a gorgeous, brilliant blue. The weather today is much nicer than it was, and although the English air is still excruciatingly cold, the sun is shining bright and causing the once dull grey colors to pop with fresh vibrancy.

Before I know it, my words have turned into incantations, then spell sequences, and then actual magical instructions. When I finally take a break, there are at least ten pages of text before me, most of which I'll need to reread in order to fully comprehend what's happening.

This is going to be a long, long spell, but it's going to be the best ritual I've ever created.

A spell for what you need, when you need it.

I begin laughing to myself, thankful and satisfied. It's been so long since I've felt that kind of creativity; I'd almost forgotten what it was like.

After taking a moment to catch my breath, I dive back in, reading from the top and I reacquaint myself with this web of incantations and instructions that I've spun.

With this incantation, that asshole parasaurolophus might actually find what he's searching for and stop being such a jerk.

I stop reading and let out a long sigh, finally realizing just how completely Snabe has consumed my thoughts.

Which also reminds me, I need to have a word with that dinosaur.

I stand up from the table and grab my coat, heading out the door and making my way down to the bard's cabin. If Dellatrix was up all night, I can only assume that Snabe was, too, but it's late enough in the afternoon to give it a shot.

I'm halfway between our cabins when I hear a loud, hollow crack ring out from somewhere within the nearby forest. It's a strange sound, and I can't quite put my finger on it until it comes echoing towards me for a second time. Someone is chopping wood.

I change course and head for the trees, only traveling a short distance before I find Snabe standing over a large stump, an axe resting by his side while his shirtless dinosaur body glistens in the afternoon light.

"Do you *ever* wear a shirt?" I call out.

The muscular parasaurolophus smiles when he sees me, then shrugs.

"Aren't you cold?" I question.

"I'm from Bristol, darling," Snabe reminds me. "You haven't seen cold yet."

The sonic spellcrafter reaches down with his bulging tattooed arm and grabs ahold of a large, fresh chunk of wood, setting it upright on the stump. He lines up his ax and then, moments later, takes a powerful swing. It's a direct hit, slicing right down through the middle and sending a chunk of wood flying out on either side in two distinct pieces.

"We ran out of wood last night," Snabe explains.

"Yeah," I reply with a laugh. "Sounds like you were up late."

Snabe shakes his head. "The motorcycles were. I went to bed early."

"Well, you're a real gentleman for getting up to chop them more wood then," I offer.

Snabe laughs. "I've been called a lot of things in my life, but gentleman isn't one of them. I'm a bad boy."

"That's not what Minerma said," I reply.

Snabe stops immediately, completely taken off guard as he rests the ax at his side. A smile creeps its way across his face. "You know Minerma?"

"She's my spellcraft agent," I explain.

Snabe seems slightly concerned by this. "Oh no. You're not a bard, too. Are you?"

"Wizard," I clarify.

Snabe nods. "A wizard, huh? You ever get wizard's block?"

"Actually, that's why I'm here," I admit. "Minerma said the island might be inspiring."

"And?" the dinosaur asks, genuinely curious.

I nod. "Made some progress this morning, actually. I'm not out of the woods yet, but I'm getting there."

"Maybe you could give me some pointers then," the bard continues. "I've been stuck for years now."

"Well... it sounded like you were making some progress on drums yesterday," I remind him.

Snabe takes a deep breath, seemingly embarrassed by his behavior in retrospect. "Yeah, that never really went anywhere."

"What about your spellsong by the water?" I question.

My words make Snabe's eyes light up suddenly, as if reminded of something very important from long ago, an idea that had been on the tip of his tongue for years and just now finally decided to pop. "That's a good one," Snabe admits. "I could never get the magic to work, though."

We stand in awkward silence for a moment, but Snabe declines to keep chopping. Instead, the dinosaur continues to take me in with his big beautiful eyes. While yesterday his leering had been nothing but off putting, his gaze now fills me with a deep warmth and attraction. I feel like he's truly seeing me now, not just passing me off as a potential new target for his bardic motorcycle harem.

"How about I give you those wizard's block pointers over dinner tonight?" I offer.

Snabe smiles. "I thought you didn't want me to take you out."

"I changed my mind," I tell him. "At least, for now."

"Fair enough, pick you up at seven?" Snabe suggests.

"Well, we live next door to each other, so calling it a pick up is a bit of a stretch," I inform the smoldering prehistoric bard. "Do you even *have* a car of your own on the island?"

"The yellow one," Snabe reminds me.

"That's Dellatrix's," I counter, "and I'm not stepping foot in that thing."

Snabe accepts this. "I'll buy us a new one. They'll deliver it before tonight."

"A new car?" I question. "You're just going to *buy* a new car?"

Snabe seems confused. "Yeah. Why not?"

I roll my eyes and turn, heading back towards my cabin. "See you at seven," I call out over my shoulder.

SNABE'S LESSON

5

Snabe's sincerity shows itself in small, strange ways, things that most people might not actually notice unless they were *really* looking deep into the heart of it all.

When the dinosaur knocks on my door at seven, I have to say that I'm kind of surprised, not just by the fact that he's managed to be punctual, but because he seems like the kind of guy who would honk his horn and expect me to come out and meet him.

Could it be that he's actually trying?

I open the door to find the dinosaur standing before me in a surprisingly well-tailored suit. It's dark and subtly striped, clearly rock and roll but also much more done up than I would've ever expected.

"You're not shirtless," I offer.

"Would you like me to take this off?" Snabe jokes.

I laugh, but then grow slightly uncomfortable when I realize he'd probably take me up on that offer if I asked.

"Your chariot awaits," Snabe tells me, opening his arms wide and gesturing towards a neon green Lamborghini that's parked right next to Dellatrix's yellow sports car.

"Wow," is all that I can say. "That's even more obnoxious than the yellow one."

Snabe remains stone faced until he just can't take it any longer, finally cracking a mischievous grin. "I'm just kidding. I've got a Jag parked around the other side of the cabin. Much classier."

I'd like to laugh, but I'm still trying to wrap my mind around how much money he must've spent on this little joke. "You bought a ridiculous Lamborghini just to mess with me?" I ask, not quite sure if I'm impressed or upset but this.

Snabe shrugs. "It's a rental."

"That's still like... five thousand dollars a day," I inform him.

"Is it?" Snabe asks. "Please keep in mind, I'm only written this way because it's a romance novel."

I let out a long sigh. "Shall we?"

The dinosaur leads the way, strolling down towards his cabin where a beautiful black Jaguar slowly comes into view. I'm not the type of girl who gives a damn about fancy cars, but I have to admit, this piece of machinery is utterly gorgeous.

Snabe presses a button and then doors slowly drift open for me, revealing an immaculately clean interior complete with that classic new car smell.

"I *did* buy this one," Snabe informs me. "Not a rental."

I hesitate, not wanting to encourage any more bad behavior but suddenly unsure of where Snabe's attitude lies. This is a nice ride, after all. "It suits you," I finally say.

The next thing I know, Snabe is pulling away from the house, making his way up the twisting dirt road and into the deep dark forest beyond. Of course, he's taking all the turns way to fast, but I'd already figure this would be the case and manage to keep my cool.

"Have you been to Captain Orion's Cove yet?" Snabe asks me.

"Yeah, the food was great," I offer, declining to get too deep into the drama that occurred after. My rental was returned home safely as promised, and the insurance covered all damages. At this point, I'd like to put all of that behind me.

"Can I play you something?" Snabe questions.

"One of your songspells?" I ask.

Snabe nods. "Just an idea I'm working on," he explains.

I can't help but find myself a little excited by the prospect of hearing a new Seven Inch Nails spell before the rest of the world. While I've slowly come to know Snabe as a person, there's still a part of me inside that remembers the posters of his face hanging on my wall at wizarding college.

It's so weird to think about that now, but the strangeness of our situation is more surreal than unpleasant.

"Play it," I say with a nod.

Snabe move his finger on the wheel, pressing a small inlayed button and then, moments later, the track begins.

A low, rumbling hum fills the car stereo, vibrating its way through my body. There's a sense of anticipation in the air, an electricity that transports me back to my days as nothing more than an excited fan. Suddenly, the drums kick in, but the rhythm is hard for me to fully get a grasp on. It starts off fine, but near the end of the beat things tumble over onto each other, as if the drummer just got too tired and gave up. This happens over and over again, a constant loop that never seems to add up to anything.

Out of the corner of my eye I can see Snabe glancing over at me, trying to read the expression on my face while I do my best to keep it together. I'm trying to give this song a fair shot, but the bizarreness of the track is making it very difficult.

Eventually, the singing kicks in, a strange, distant moan that feels disconnected from the rest of the music. The constant drone from the top of the song is still wailing away, but at this point it has gone completely out of tune with the vocals, causing me to literally wince as it crosses my ears.

This goes on for a good minute before I suddenly realize exactly what's going on. I reach out and turn down the stereo.

"Good one," I offer Snabe sarcastically. "Now where's the real songspell?"

The dinosaur bard looks confused, but I'm still not buying it. "Did it work?" he questions, trying to get a good look at me. "Your eyes are supposed to change color for the next hour."

"You got me once with the fake car, but you're not gonna get me again with a fake spell," I continue. "Do you really have a new track or what?"

Snabe scrunches his face up. "That bad, huh?"

I realize now that he's being utterly sincere.

A wave of embarrassment washes over my body as I sit back into my passenger seat and stare out the front windshield. "I'm sorry," I tell him, trying desperately to cover up for my mistake. "Maybe I just wasn't listening closely. Let me hear it again."

The handsome parasaurolophus bard just shakes his head.

"That was really bad," I finally admit, my words eventually evolving into uncontrollable laughter. "Didn't you go to some fancy wizarding school for rich bards?"

The next thing I know, Snabe is laughing, too, the two of us cackling wildly as we continue towards town. In the midst of this, I suddenly realize it's the first time I've completely let my guard down around Snabe. There's no part of me that sees this dinosaur as some arrogant asshole romance character, nor a famous rockstar bard, nor a billionaire playboy or a distant parody of some wizardly school teacher. Right now, Snabe is just Snabe, the same sweet guy that Minerma knew growing up on the island.

"You know, the motorcycles said they loved it," the handsome parasaurolophus informs me. "Dellatrix actually called the spell *mind expanding*. Her eyes changed color, but later I noticed her taking out some contacts."

"I'm sure she did," I reply.

Snabe lets out a long sigh. He knows exactly what I'm thinking, so I decline to say it out loud. "I get it," Snabe finally offers. "I know."

"What about that thing you were playing down on the beach?" I question. "That was gorgeous."

Snabe nods. "It is, but I've got a little confession about that spell. It's not new."

'It's not?" I reply, slightly confused. "I know your old record like the back of my hand, and I've never heard that one before."

Snabe raises an eyebrow. "So you *are* a super fan! I knew it!"

"Maybe," I retort.

Snabe shrugs. "I've been working on that spell for years. It kind of… follows me around. It's so beautiful, but any time I try putting vocals over the top of it they're just not good enough. It's like, I've got this beautiful painting, but whenever I try to finish it, I just make a mess."

"What does it do?" I question.

"My heart knows but… my brain doesn't, yet. Does that make sense?" he offers.

As a fellow spellcrafter, Snabe's words hit close to home. Sometimes spells are just feelings that bubble up from deep inside you; the more you try and lock them down, the more they drift away. "That was a big problem for me when I was crafting my first big spell after wizarding school," I offer. "I was just about halfway done, and I knew where I wanted it to go, but every time I tried to shape its direction it lost its power. I started to second-guess every single word of the incantation. Honestly, I got pretty close to giving up entirely." I consider this comment for a moment. "God damn. My life would be so different."

"What did you do?" Snabe suddenly blurts. I glance over and realize now that he's hanging on every word, completely entranced by my tale of wizardly spellcrafting peril.

"I pushed through it," I inform him, proudly. "I realized that I didn't have faith in myself, in my talent, in my work, so I went out of my way to change that. I looked inward and said 'I *am* a bad ass, and I made a bad ass spell.' Once I realized that, it worked perfectly."

Snabe nods, but he says nothing. I can tell that my words are hitting close to home, but he's not yet ready to admit it. He's a dinosaur who, by all outside appearances, has confidence and swagger to spare, but deep down at his core, Snabe is still terrified that he's worthless.

"Sometimes, when I'm stuck, I just start writing incantations and let my mind speak for itself," I continue. "I don't second-guess anything, or look back at it until I've had some time away. I just go for it. Maybe you should try that. Just let the raw magic out."

Snabe nods in acceptance. "Maybe I should."

We spend the rest of the car ride in silence, but not awkward or uncomfortable. The feeling is actually quite warm and inviting, like I'm exactly where I'm supposed to be.

Eventually, we arrive at the restaurant, pulling up and parking out front in the same spot I'd taken yesterday. We climb out and head down the nearby alley, but before we get very far, Snabe slides up and puts his scaly green arm around me.

It's a forward gesture, especially given the fact that I was reluctant to come on this date in the first place, but I don't move away. My first instinct is to pull back, of course, but once I get past my initial shock, Snabe's presence is incredibly satisfying. It's been a long time since I've felt this protected, and although I don't think I can trust him with my heart, Snabe's large prehistoric frame feels quite welcome against mine. I nuzzle into the muscular parasaurolophus, and he pulls me close.

This wordless exchange only lasts a brief moment, however, because the next thing I know, we're arriving at the restaurant door. Snabe opens it up for me and then waves me inside.

The waitress who'd served me before is here, and her eyes go wide when she sees me.

"You're back!" the woman shouts excitedly, strolling over to us. "How's the car?"

"It's great now," I explain. "Just the tires were damaged. Easy fix."

"Good, good," the waitress replies with a nod, then turns to face Snabe. Her expression quickly erupts into even more of a wild-eyed grin. "And you! Where have you been these days?"

"Hey Gobby, just working," Snabe offers with a smile. The two of them hug warmly.

"Getting into trouble?" she questions.

Snabe smiles. "A little bit. Trying not to. I was written as a bad boy after all."

Gobby leads us over to the same table I'd taken before, the corner spot with a beautiful view of the cove as it spreads out in either direction. Now that night has fallen, there's not quite as much to see, but the stars twinkling above us are more than enough to momentarily take my breath away. Honestly, I don't know if I've ever seen the sky so clearly, the big city light typically doing their best to pollute my view.

Gobby leaves us to look over our menus, but I can't help remain transfixed by the brilliant night sky outside, a whole world of astral dust that I've never had a chance to notice. It's so strange to think that these stars and planets, entire galaxies even, have been hanging above my head this whole time, and yet I was never quite in the right position to see them.

Snabe follows my gaze out the window, joining me in this moment of cosmic awe.

"It's hard to imagine struggling for inspiration when there's so much raw magic and beauty in the universe," I finally offer.

"Tell me about it," the dinosaur replies. "I think our talk is going to help, though."

I glance back down at the muscular bard, his parasaurolophus frame large and imposing before me. If I didn't already know him, I'd find the dinosaur to be quite intimidating, even for someone as blunt and confident as myself. His suit may be well cut tonight, but it still manages to show off just how toned his body is, the man's bulging arms pressed tightly against their inner fabric. Most of Snabe's tattoos have been covered, but just enough of them can be seen peeking out from under the collar of his shirt.

Maybe there's a beauty within Snabe's conflicted personality that's perfect exactly the way it is, like these gorgeous stars that've hung above my head without me ever finding the right time to notice them.

I smile, allowing the dinosaur's words to simmer in the air between us without a response. Instead, I quietly look down at my menu, perusing the food and allowing myself to take in this moment without any pretense. I've been so wrapped up in my creative mission during this trip, that I haven't really had a chance to just sit back and enjoy myself.

Unlike this afternoon, the restaurant around us is humming with activity. Patrons crowd nearly every other table, but I suppose when there's only two places to eat on this island you're bound to do good business in the evenings.

Snabe has noticed the other diners around us, as well, but his focus seems to be much more pointed than mine. I follow that man's gaze to see that he's watching intently while a nearby table orders from Gobby. The waitress is just trying to do her job, but the men snapping at her with sloppy enthusiasm are just barely coherent enough to function.

Finally, Gobby returns to our table.

"It's busy tonight," the woman offers with a smile. "You two know what you'd like?"

"What was that all about?" the parasaurolophus questions with grave concern.

"They've had a little too much chocolate milk to drink," Gobby explains. "I thought about kicking them out, but we need all the business we can get."

"It looks like things are doing pretty damn well," I butt in.

Gobby nods. "The dinner rush doesn't make up for dead afternoons, though. Like I said, we've gotta take what we can get."

This seems like a reasonable answer, and I accept it, but I can tell that Snabe is still intensely focused on the other table's obnoxious diners.

I order the cod spaghetti again from Gobby, and Snabe somehow manages to pull himself together enough to ask for a rare steak. The waitress leaves.

"You look like you want to punch those guys in the face," I finally inform my date.

"Not yet," he tells me. "We'll see if they mess with Gobby much more."

On one hand, there's something kind of sweet about Snabe's protective nature of this innocent, older lady. Gobby is certainly kind and caring and, from what I can tell, the situation with her sick daughter appears to be utterly tragic, but I also get the feeling that part of this comes down to the fact that Snabe just wants to fight somebody.

I can't let myself forget that the layers within Snabe's personality are made up of both darkness and light. He is a complicated man; a bad boy.

I notice now that Snabe has started to hum a little tune under his breath, a familiar incantation that I remember from wizarding school. He's manifesting a short burst of subternatural speed.

When Gobby strolls by the other table again, one of the drunken men reaches out and grabs her by the arm, stopping her in her tracks and simultaneously knocking over his half-filled glass of chocolate milk, which shatters across the dining room floor.

"Look what you made me do now!" the man cries out, staggering to his feet.

He doesn't get very far.

The second these events begin to fall into place, Snabe is already out of his chair and moving towards the commotion like a literal bolt of lightning. The parasaurolophus has a singular focus, the rest of the world completely blocked out as he marches through the restaurant. The next thing I know, the handsome dinosaur's swinging a powerful fist, connecting like a speeding truck with the side of the drunk man's head.

The drunk goes down instantly, knocked out cold before he even has a chance to slam against the wooden floor below with a loud thud.

"Alright motherfucker," the drunk's equally intoxicated friend blurts, climbing out of his seat and putting his hands up in a vague boxing stance. The man begins to move back and forth, displaying a basic knowledge of how to fight.

Unfortunately, this knowledge doesn't seem to help him out much.

Snabe waits patiently for a few seconds, enjoying his temporary supernatural speed. Suddenly, and without warning, the dinosaur takes his second swing. This one connects just as hard as the first, slamming the intoxicated patron hard in the face and sending him tumbling back against the wall.

Now everything becomes breathtakingly silent, the entire room watching as Snabe stands over these men triumphantly. The situation feels both heroic and awkward, nobody quite sure how to react to the violence that just exploded before their very eyes.

Snabe finally gets back to business while the restaurant remains still, reaching down and picking up one of the knocked cold drunks over his shoulder. This physical feat is even more impressive than his brawling skills, to be honest. I'm well aware of Snabe's large, parasaurolophus form, but these two other men are just as big. Still, Snabe seems to have no problem hoisting the guy up and carrying him out the door of the restaurant.

Moments later, Snabe returns for the next man, lifting him up and carrying him into the darkness.

When Snabe come back for the last time, the restaurant is still completely silent, every eye in the place focused squarely on the bad boy dinosaur in the dark suit with blood on his scaly green knuckles.

Snabe strolls over to Gobby, putting a comforting hand on her shoulder. "Sorry about that," he says, quietly. "Just put their tab on ours. I'll cover it."

The dinosaur then continues onward, returning to his chair across from me as if nothing happened.

"You've got blood on your hands, and your collar," I observe.

Snabe nods. "One of them got clocked pretty good there. He'll be fine. They're just outside walking it off."

"Is that so?" I question, my eyebrows raised skeptically.

Snabe shrugs. "Sitting it off, maybe."

The handsome bard suddenly notices that the patrons around us are still staring in complete silence. He turns his attention to the room. "Sorry about that everyone!" Snabe calls out. "Everything's fine. You can all go back to eating now."

Slowly but surely, people start returning to the food before them.

"Am I supposed to be impressed by that?" I question. "Violence isn't a huge turn on for me."

Snabe shakes his head. "No. They just need to think about how they treat Gobby when they come in here. I'm not here to impress anyone. You've gotta remember that bad boy characters walk the line between appropriate and inappropriate. It's for the readers just as much as it is for Gobby."

I have to admit, while I'd like to pretend that Snabe's aggression didn't turn me on, there's something to be said for a man who takes charge of a situation so passionately. At least he was fighting for a good reason.

He just seemed a little *too* excited about it.

"Where did you learn to fight like that?" I question.

"The pubs back home can get a little rowdy on occasion," the man informs me with a smirk.

I shake my head. Snabe's methods were direct and refined, not a single bit of energy wasted while he disposed of his targets. This wasn't a fight carried out by a dinosaur who has accidently fallen into one or two drunken brawls over the years.

"You were way too good at that," I inform the parasaurolophus. "I'm a wizard. I notice these small things. Fighting is in your blood."

Snabe nods. "I can feel the meta layers of reality vibrating so I know we're on track. As a bad boy character, this kind of thing is bound to happen, and you're bound to be both disgusted and impressed. The thing is, this isn't just a romance, it's also a parody, and a loose one. Chuck has very literal understanding of the source material."

"What source material?" I question, narrowing my eyes. "You always start talking like this and I have no idea what it means."

"I'm sorry," Snabe offers. "Metamagic provides me with a... let's say, *broader* point of view than most. I guess what I'm saying is, while romance novels tend to peddle the idea that toxic bad boys can change, in reality you probably want to avoid someone like me. I'd be a shitty boyfriend and a shitty professor."

"A shitty professor?" I blurt. "What are you even talking about?"

"Sorry," the parasaurolophus offers with a laugh. "Let's get back to the fight."

"You know, you can turn these feelings of aggression into inspiration," I offer. "That's what spellcrafting is for. That's what *art* is for."

"It's easier to be a bad boy," Snabe informs me.

"I never said it was easy," I counter.

Before I know it, my hand has crept its way across the table, meeting Snabe's in the middle. He places his scaly claw over mine, a pleasant shiver pulsing through my whole frame the second that our skin meets.

This moment is both terrifying and intoxicating. I know that he's a dangerous parasaurolophus to get close to, that his issues as a meta-aware character are much too deep for me to sort through on my own, but the prospect of trying my damnedest seems like a roller coaster ride that just might be worth it in the end.

Still, how the hell was any of this supposed to work? Snabe currently has two fuck buddy motorcycles waiting for him back at the cabin, awful machines that he doesn't seem to mind having around. Regardless of how hard I try to connect to the dinosaur, he might just never be ready for someone like me. Maybe he likes a life that's constantly hovering on the edge of complete and utter collapse.

I pull my hand away, a gesture that Snabe takes note of, but doesn't address.

Moments later, our food arrives. Me and my handsome green companion immediately dig in, the stress of the day's conflict building us up to a state of ravenous hunger. The meal is absolutely incredible, just as satisfying as the last time I was here, but in an entirely new way.

"You're a lot different than the women I usually meet," Snabe informs me between bites of his bloody rare steak.

"Oh yeah?" I ask. "How's that?"

Snabe thinks about my question for a moment, as if he initially started talking about it without knowing where he was headed.

"Well, you don't seem to like me," the parasaurolophus laughs. "The women I meet are typically falling all over themselves at this point."

I scoff. "I like you!"

"Then why pull away," Snabe questions.

I glance down at his hand again, suddenly wondering the same thing.

"You've already got a girlfriend," I remind Snabe. "Two of them, actually."

"Dellatrix and Braco?" the creature says with a laugh, rolling his eyes. "They're not my girlfriends. Those are my motorcycles."

"They're more than that," I continue.

Snabe has no response to this.

"I'm not interested in something like that," I let him know. "I've got nothing against it, and I've done it before. Just not right now."

The parasaurolophus sits back in his chair, chewing his food and gazing out though the window at the dark water below. The moon casts a long yellow line across the moving waves, shimmering beautifully.

"What if I sent them home tomorrow?" Snabe questions.

I laugh. "Then maybe I'd consider a second date. *Maybe*. The thing is, you're not gonna do that."

The man doesn't protest this, something that I completely expected, yet it still causes a strange surge of pain to erupt deep down within my heart.

"You're right," the dinosaur finally replies. "The story's not even halfway over. It can't be that easy."

Suddenly, a figure is standing next to the table, drawing the attention of Snabe and me upward. It's Braco.

"Dellatrix needs you," the motorcycle blurts, her eyes frantic and her stark blonde hair a tangled, damp mess. "She's in the hospital."

MEETING IN THE WOODS

6

The second we pull up to the hospital, if you could call it that, Snabe is jumping out of the car and heading for the front doors. His Jaguar is taking up two spots, but thankfully the lot is almost completely empty and we don't appear to be in anyone's way. Frankly, I'm blown away by the fact that this island even *has* a hospital, regardless of that fact that it appears to be no more than one story, with only four rooms, and is located on a small piece of property at the edge of town.

I follow briskly behind Snabe, tightly wrapping my coat around my body as the wickedly cold air whips across my skin. Braco is with us as well, and she glances over at me with a strange look that I can't quite put my finger on.

"Where is she?" Snabe demands to know as we enter the lobby, a question that would probably be met with confusion anywhere else, but makes perfect sense thanks to the fact that there's currently only one patient.

"Just down the hall and to the right," the nurse tells us from behind her desk.

The three of us continue onward, quickly ending up in the doorway of a small hospital room where a doctor is waiting. Dellatrix's lying next to him in a tiny white bed, covered in thick blankets and looking pale. There's a massive, red welt on the motorcycle's forehead, so bruised and bloody that it's swelled into a massive bump.

It would probably be worse if it weren't for the fact that Dellatrix is gently holding an ice pack against it.

During the car ride, Braco was only able to give us a vague description of what happened, her story quickly cut short by the fact that the hospital was less than a mile away. All we know is that Dellatrix fell in the water, and Braco had to drag her out.

"What happened?" Snabe asks Dellatrix, but the doctor interjects.

"I'm Doctor Abaso," he says, extending his hand. "You must be Snabe."

Snabe ignores the doctor completely, continuing towards Dellatrix and taking a seat on the stool by her bed. "Are you okay?"

Dellatrix nods and smiles. "Of course, baby."

Finally, Snabe turns his attention back to the doctor. "I'm sorry about that. Yes, I'm Snabe."

"Good," the doctor offers with a smile. "Dellatrix had a pretty bad fall, as you can see from the bruise on her head. I did an x-ray and her skull is fine, as well as her tires, brake pads and engine, but she suffered a rather large concussion, so I'd recommend a lot of rest."

"Aren't you supposed to *not* sleep after a concussion?" I question.

"That's only for humans, motorcycles are different," the doctor explains. "After a blow like this, the brain needs rest. That's not all she's been through tonight, though."

"I slipped on the dock," Dellatrix finally croaks. "I'm so stupid. We shouldn't have been down there rolling around in the dark. I was just puttering along and then suddenly I was falling. I can't remember anything after that."

"Back on the beach and I heard a loud crack," Braco continues, picking up the story from there. "When I called out for her, she didn't respond, so I walked out onto the dock to look. I didn't see Dellatrix at first, and then I suddenly spotted her sinking under the water. I thought she was dead, honestly."

"Oh my god," Snabe blurts.

Braco can't help but smile at this outburst, loving the attention but trying her hardest not to let on. It doesn't slip past me, though.

"I dove into the water," Braco continues. "It was so cold. I couldn't get Braco up onto the dock, so I had to drag her all the way back to the beach."

"That's where I woke up," Dellatrix replies dramatically.

"Both motorcycles are going to be fine," the doctor affirms, "I've provided them with ample doses of healing potion, but rest is very important at this point. Dellatrix was in the water for quite a long time, but there doesn't appear to be any permanent engine damage."

"I'm just so lucky Braco was there," Dellatrix says, laying it on thick.

The motorbikes look to one another and exchange glances in a way that the guys don't seem to notice or mind, but makes me immediately start to question the validity of their story. Sure, it's believable enough that someone could've slipped and fallen on that dock in the dark, but there's something about the way these events are laid out that doesn't quite add up to me.

Not to mention, the timing of everything is just a little too strange to ignore. Dellatrix threatens me over Snabe, but I go out with him anyway, and the next thing I know she's in a life or death situation that demands his attention. All the while, Braco gets to look like a hero for once, which is just the icing on the cake.

Of course, there's nothing I can say or do about any of this without looking jealous, insane or both.

"I'm so sorry," Snabe sighs, leaning over the bed and hugging his wounded bird.

Dellatrix and me make eye contact over Snabe's shoulder as this happens, and for a split second her expression changes to one of smirking arrogance. The motorcycle gives me a mischievous wink, but it disappears just as quickly as it arrives.

"I want to go home," Dellatrix coos in Snabe's ear.

The muscular and protective dinosaur bard turns towards Doctor Abaso. "Is that alright?"

The doctor nods. "She's ready to leave, just make sure to keep her warm and give her lots of oil. Make sure there's air in those tires. She needs to sleep immediately after arriving home, and should spend the next few days in bed."

"Not a problem," Dellatrix offers, a perfectly reasonable commentary on just how exhausted she is, if it weren't for the fact that she reaches out and brushes Snabe's claw when she says this.

The next few minutes are spent signing Dellatrix out and helping her to the car, painstakingly assuring that everything is set up exactly how she likes it. She ends up riding in the black Jag with Snabe, while I'm forced to transfer over to the disgusting yellow two-seater that I swore I'd never ride in.

Braco takes the wheel and we head back to our respective cabins in total silence, our eyes completely transfixed on the winding road before us while wading deep in our own very separate thoughts.

For the first time since I arrived here on the island, I actually want to leave.

Sure, I was frustrated, and upset, and angry. I went from thinking Snabe was a complete asshole, to a handsome troublemaker, to a lost cause. But at no point did I actually want to leave this place that I knew was destined to eventually inspire me.

Ironically, now that the incantations have started to flow, I want to get as far away from here as possible. There's no comfort for me on the island, no ease, but I suppose that's a small sacrifice to make for spellcraft.

I still haven't come up with anything that's good enough for Minerma to take a look at, but it's coming. The ritual has started to fall into place.

Meanwhile, I've been avoiding any contact with Snabe's cabin, and they seem to be avoiding any contact with me. It's only been a few days since Dellatrix's accident, but things have been relatively quiet, not a single note of thunderous bardic music floating up from down below.

This afternoon, I've decided to get out of the house and take a hike up into the hillside. I'm not far from the cabins below, but just one or two steps past the tree line will transport you into a place of lush wilderness, thick trunks shooting up from all around you while massive, dark green ferns spill over from every rocky crevice.

I bring along my wand, using it to cast *treemus passious*. This spell creates a well-groomed trail through any non-magical woods, the plants separating to create a magical path between the walker and their destination.

Sometimes, however, the trail this spell manifests can be quite winding. My hike is steep, taking me up the hillside in a series of switchbacks.

I'm an outsider in this majestic place, but I see that as a privilege. This is a secret moment that I'll never share, something that can forever remain between the trees and me.

At least, that's what I thought.

Suddenly, there's a loud snap from behind me, a branch cracking into pieces under a heavy foot.

I spin around to find Snabe walking up the path. He stops when our eyes meet.

"What are you doing out here?" I finally question. "Something tells me this isn't a coincidence."

Snabe laughs, his sharp-toothed smile immediately getting to work on my cold exterior. I can sense my initial defenses already melting away, no match for his rugged, prehistoric charm. He's wearing black pants and a heather grey T-shirt that seems perfectly crafted for his incredible, muscular body, hugging his broad chest in just the right way.

"You're mad at me," Snabe finally offers. "I cast a songspell to glance at the pages I'm not written into."

I draw in a deep breath, taking my time as I determine how to react to this. Truth be told, I'm absolutely angry with Snabe, but I'm not exactly sure why. The dinosaur makes no secret about how difficult he is to deal with, and any emotional attachment that I've developed is my responsibility, not his.

I'm well aware of this, and yet for some reason the idea of him lying around down there with those two terrible motorcycles makes me frustrated to the very core.

Instead of saying that, however, I change the subject. "How's Dellatrix?" I ask.

"She's... okay," Snabe offers. "I wish I knew more healing spells, but my training lies in metamagic. Seems like she should be doing better by now, but then again she was in that water for a pretty long time."

"You don't say," I reply, trying my best to hide my disdain, but doing a terrible job of it.

"I've been working," Snabe informs me, his yellow eyes suddenly flickering with excitement. "Your talk the other day really helped me. Honestly. I saw you hiking up this way and I needed to come thank you."

"Our talk?" I question.

"In the car," Snabe continues. "You told me to channel my frustration into my spellcraft. I mean, it's seems so obvious, but for some reason I could never really do that before. Any time things got too personal, I'd just shut it down, but you encouraged me to push through."

"The acoustic song?" I ask.

Snabe nods, smiling wide. "I finished the arrangement and tracked some incantations over it. They're not finished, but it's a good start."

Finally, my cold exterior breaks. "That's... wonderful," I tell him.

Snabe steps towards me, closer and closer until we are right up next to each other. He takes my hand and then reaches into his pocket, pulling out a tiny thumb drive that he places in my palm. I close my fingers around it.

"Be very, very careful with that," Snabe explains.

I nod. "What is it?"

"A rough draft of the songspell," the muscular bard informs me. "Just a quick recording of that song. I'm calling it *Moonbeamus Metamalium* for now."

"Sounds nice," I tell him, immediately remembering the way that the yellow light of the moon had reflected off of the water while we had dinner together, the shimmering beauty of its form stretching across the waves.

I put the thumb drive into my pocket.

"Is that it?" I question.

I suddenly realize that our bodies are just barely touching one another now, the tension between us hanging heavy and thick in the air.

"I don't know," Snabe replies with a smirk. "Is it?"

My breathing heaving, I suddenly find my body surging with lust, completely taken by the bad boy dinosaur's powerful presence. He may be endlessly frustrating, but right now that's the last thing on my mind.

"What are you waiting for?" I whisper.

Suddenly, I'm kissing Snabe deeply, or lips meeting in an explosion of passion. Before I can even fully comprehend what's happening, my hands are roving across his dinosaur body, tracing the curves of his muscular chest that I've spent so long mapping with my eyes. His large prehistoric frame is even more impressive under the palms of my hands, every single inch of the parasaurolophus toned to absolute perfection.

"What am I doing?" I gasp.

"Taking what you want," Snabe informs me.

I have no idea if this is the truth. I'm not interested in joining the dinosaur's motorcycle harem, not that there's anything wrong with that, but the cravings bubbling up within me would say otherwise.

Of course, one moment of passion doesn't have to be anything other than just that, and all these things can be sorted out later. Right now, consequences are the last thing I want to think about.

I push any logic out of my mind, instead focusing on the powerful cravings that continue to build within me. I'm completely overwhelmed with animalistic desire, wanting nothing more than to give myself over to Snabe completely.

I quickly pull the dinosaur's shirt up over the top of his head, tossing it to the side and revealing his brawny torso in all of its glory. Moments later, my top is coming off too, revealing the cute maroon and gold sports bra underneath.

I also carefully remove my glasses, setting them on a nearby stump.

Pushing him backwards, I continue to make out with Snabe until his rear comes to rest against a massive tree trunk, spiraling up above us in a cascade of long, sweeping branches. I'm clawing at the parasaurolophus now, my fingers drifting lower and lower until, eventually, they reach his belt buckle and tear it open. I swiftly move on to Snabe's zipper, dropping to my knees and yanking down his waistband.

Suddenly, Snabe's enormous member has erupted out into my face, a dark green strap-on with a thickness unlike anything I have ever seen. It's so enormous that it actually startles me, staring down this bardic python as it sways in the fresh forest air.

"Before we go any farther, this is my cock," the dinosaur informs me. "Don't call it a strap-on, don't even think of it as a strap-on. This is my dick. Understood?"

"You've got a huge cock," I reply with a smile.

I open wide and take Snabe's dick between my lips, bobbing my head up and down across his length while the dinosaur above me moans loudly, his voice echoing out across the woods. I'll be perfectly honest, it's been a while since I've done anything like this, but I pick things up again quickly.

Snabe is clearly enjoying himself, his head tilted back as a long, satisfied groan escapes his lips. With the large tree positioned firmly behind him, the parasaurolophus has nowhere to squirm to, nowhere to pull back and release the pleasure that is now bubbling up within. I can feel his gorgeous abs flexing and releasing above me, struggling to adjust to the cascade of sensations that are now being thrust upon him.

Suddenly, Snabe takes me by the shoulders and pushes me back a bit, then helps me to my feet. "You're too good to me," he coos. "Let me be good to you."

"But you're a bad boy," a reply with a laugh. "You're telling me you can be good, too?"

"For you, I can try," Snabe affirms, his tone momentarily shifting towards the serious.

The dinosaur takes me with his massive claws and carefully slips my hiking shorts down, along with my panties. I step out of them as Snabe looks me over, smiling wide at the thought of whatever he has planned.

Suddenly, Snabe is using his enormous, muscular arms to lift me up in the air, spinning me around so that now *my* back is pressed up against the tree. The only difference, of course, is that I'm five and a half feet or so off of the ground.

"You can touch it," I explain, "and you can suck it, but call it what it is: not a dick. That's my clit."

My legs over both of Snabe's scaly green shoulders, I now find him with his face buried deep in my crotch, the man's wet tongue softly lapping across my most sensitive areas.

"Oh my god," I gasp, my face flushed red from the incredible sensations that are pulsing through my body.

Snabe appears to know exactly what he's doing, alternating between long, slow sucks and a series of staccato flicks from the tip of his tongue. He somehow knows exactly how my body is going to react, pushing me forward and then pulling me back in a never-ending series of tension and release. I grab the back of his head and pull him even closer, desperately running my fingers through the dinosaur's long dark hair.

Up here in the air I feel even more disconnected from responsibility or consequences, completely free to sexually express myself with the help of this beautiful lover. While the woman I used to be still haunts the forest floor below, I've graduated to the trees. My animalistic desires have brought me even closer to nature than ever before, the fresh influence I'd been so desperately looking for.

Or maybe I'm just having a really good time. Sometimes, as a wizard, it's easy to get carried away with the metaphors I see in the world. A good fuck is beautiful, and sexy, and sensual, but it's also fun.

Maybe it took a guy like Snabe to help me fully realize that.

By now, the first simmers of orgasm have already started to bubble up within me. I push into them, allowing these feelings to consume me as Snabe keeps up the pace with the confident bob of his head. It's a lot to take, but I refuse to turn away, forcing myself to accept these powerful sensations head on.

The beautiful orgasmic warmth starts at the pit of my stomach, then slowly begins to make its way out across my body, blossoming with tendrils of aching pleasure. I'm trembling wildly as it moves down my arms and legs, filling me up with a potent ache and causing my eyes to roll back into my head. I'm breathing heavy, my heart slamming hard in my chest as I edge closer and closer to the edge of climax.

"Oh my god," I groan, my voice cascading down the tree covered hillside. "Oh my god! Oh my god!"

The pressure continues to build until, finally, the dam breaks. I throw back my head and let out a howl of pleasure, my scream echoing out around us and causing a plume of nearby birds to erupt from their tree.

In this moment, Snabe and I are fully connected to one another; I single entity drawn together by forces much bigger than ourselves. Sure, our paths have twisted and turned to get here, but they make so much sense once they finally meet.

When the sensation finally passes, Snabe swallows my load then begins to lower me down. We're not through with each other yet, though. Before my feet have a chance to touch the ground, my muscular lover allows me to wrap my legs around his waist, hovering with expect precision above his enormous rod.

"Can you go longer?" the dinosaur questions.

"*Sexualis Secondus,*" I announce proudly, waving my wand in the air.

The two of us watch as my clit begins to swell again.

"Incredible," Snabe remarks with a grin.

"That's not my ass, though," I begin.

"I know," the parasaurolophus offers, cutting me off. "You don't even need to say it."

Now at the same height, our gaze is locked together, eyes burning deep into one another's soul. We're so close that our foreheads are touching, the sweaty hair tangling as our heavy breathing starts to sync. Moments later, Snabe lowers me down, impaling my body across his mammoth shaft.

The first thing that strikes me is the incredible feeling of fullness. I've been with plenty of men before, but never had their member fit so perfectly within my pussy. If I was any less aroused, in fact, it might be too tight, but in this state of belligerent lust the insertion is exactly what it should be.

Snabe immediately gets to work grinding up into me, using his hips in a series of rhythmic swoops as I hold on tight.

The sex is incredible, but even more incredible is the feeling of closeness that I get when our bare skin is pressed so tightly. As emotionally intimate as me and Snabe have grown, our physical connection has been completely barren up until now. Suddenly, I'm receiving it all at once, and the overwhelming sensation of Snabe's touch is everything that I hoped it would be.

Our heaving bodies start slow and then gradually begin to speed up, connecting in ways that I never could've imagined possible. The dinosaur has a beautiful confidence to his rhythm, a true bard even when his instrument is sexual gratification.

It's not long before the orgasmic sensations begin to blossom up within me yet again, only this time the feeling has spread out across a second body. Snabe and me have merged into a single entity, the movements of our writhing frames perfectly in sync as that familiar, warm feelings continues to build within us.

I can immediately tell that this moment is not just another random fuck for Snabe. There is something else brewing here, something that can only be attained when two opposing, but equally powerful, forces collide.

"It's so good," I begin to stammer, the words falling limply from my mouth in a blissed out mantra, repeating over and over again as they escalate in volume.

Soon enough, Snabe is moaning as well, our cries blending in perfect harmony. The parasaurolophus doesn't let up for a second, slamming into me now as my fingers dig deep into his scaly back.

Suddenly, the two of us throw our heads back in unison, letting out parallel screams of passion that go on and on for what seems like forever.

When the feeling of orgasm finally passes, Snabe sets me down once more.

I begin to gather my clothes, pulling them on while my eyes remain transfixed on Snabe's perfect, tattoo covered physique. I'm still having trouble believing this dinosaur is real.

"That was incredible," the muscular bard tells me as he finishes clothing himself.

"Just the workout I was looking for," I joke, still high from my recent orgasm.

The two of us finish getting dressed and then pause, standing for a moment as we continue to come to terms with what just happened. Without saying a word we come together again, only this time we do nothing more than hug.

Our arms wrapped around one another's bodies, we simply exist in each other's presence for a while, listening to the wind as it pulses through the trees and the soft, distant sound of the ocean as it laps along the shore.

"Don't think this changes anything," I finally inform him. "I'm still not interested in being a part of your little crew."

"I know," the dinosaur tells me with a halfhearted smile.

"Do you care?" I question.

Snabe sighs. "Yeah. I do."

"And?" I continue.

The single word goes unanswered, drifting away in the wind.

Eventually, Snabe and me release one another and turn to head back down the hill. The purpose of that hike was to get my heart pumping and my inspiration flowing, and although the route I'd planned remains incomplete, that's exactly what has happened. I'm ready to create, ready to take these feelings that swirl around inside of me and spill them out onto the page.

When Snabe and I exit the tree line, we instantly spot two figures standing over by his cabin. It's Braco and Dellatrix, the latter wrapped tightly in a warm blanket while she stares daggers deep into my soul. It's clear they're trying to be intimating, to stake their claim after hearing what must've been a hell of a commotion from up in the woods. I don't mind.

"Hey there!" I offer with a wink and a wave.

The motorcycles refuse to respond.

I turn my attention back to Snabe as our path's split. "I can't wait to listen to this songspell," I tell him, loud enough for Dellatrix to hear. "I'll let you know what I think."

Snabe nods as the expression on Dellatrix's face sinks to an even more depressing depth. I can see now that she's barely holding herself together, but before Dellatrix has a chance to collapse completely, the furious woman turns and rolls back into the darkness of their cabin.

I continue on my way, waiting until I've gotten back inside before breaking out in a full-on smile. I know that what just happened between Snabe and I will only serve to complicate things, and it was probably a terrible idea from the start, but I'll be damned if I didn't enjoy myself.

My biggest concern, of course, is that no matter how hard I try, Snabe continues to work his way deeper into my heart. There's a connection between us that refuses to come undone, slowly pulling us closer and closer together.

Now that we've had sex, will that fascination finally be quelled? Or will things just continue to grow even more heated than before?

I sit down at the kitchen table; letting these romantic thoughts bloom out across my mind. I picture a myriad of different futures with Snabe, what it would be like to travel the world with him, or to settle down and start a family.

It only takes a moment for me to snap out of it.

Of course this will be the end of it, I realize, because Snabe and me can never truly be a real item. Regardless of how attracted I am to the dinosaur, or how much he tries to release the sweet soul hidden behind his angsty bad boy exterior, he's currently not in any position to have a functioning, adult relationship.

And I've got a hit spell to craft.

Still, I can't ever seem to push Snabe out of my mind entirely. Even when I'm deep in the zone, my fingers flying wildly across the keyboard, Snabe is still hidden somewhere deep down within the subliminal recesses of my brain.

I get a few paragraphs of incantations down and then stop abruptly, realizing now that ritual I'm developing has more to do with metamagic than I thought. It's almost as those this whole thing is happening because of something outside of my control, outside of the very fabric of this reality. Maybe some author in another dimension set forth a chain of events that's channeling energy into my very spell.

Or maybe Snabe's preference for metamagic is just rubbing off on me.

I'm suddenly reminded of the song he gave me, I pull out the dinosaur's thumb drive and push it into my laptop's USB port, watching as the file suddenly appears on screen. I double click the icon, then lean back into my chair as sweet sound begins to wash over me.

I recognize the first few acoustic guitar chords immediately, their pattern stuck firmly in my mind ever since hearing them down by the water on that cool evening not long ago. The sweeping tones send chills through my body, drawing me in.

Usually, I like to listen to music while I'm doing something else, whether it's writing or cleaning or driving in my car. This songspell, however, demands my full attention. It's sparse and beautiful, pulling the listener in without making a big scene about it.

The second Snabe's vocal incantation starts, my breath catches in my throat. Up until this point, I'd only known this spellsong as an instrumental piece, but now that it's presented with a soft, delicate vocal over the top, the song takes on a completely new life. Honestly, I can barely believe this is Snabe.

The spell itself begins to take effect. I see line after line of black and white bars stacked on top of one another, running horizontally and stretching on for what seems like forever. At first I'm not quite sure what they are, but as I stare longer I realize that these bars are actually words, long beautiful descriptions of exactly what's going on around me.

I see the previous paragraph, along with the one that comes after this. I see my whole world for what it is, a glorious piece of art, and because of this realization I realize that I'm separate from the story that I'm written into. The very nature of metamagic means that my mind, my soul, is separate from this story.

I am me, regardless of the framework that I've suddenly appeared in.

When the song finally finishes, I wipe a single tear away from the corner of my eye. I had no idea I was crying, my mind elsewhere as the songspell flowed over and through me. Although it's clear from the recording that this is nothing more than a rough sketch of the track to come, I can already tell that it's exactly what Snabe needs if he wants to push Seven Inch Nails back into the limelight. It's one of those songspells that is utterly undeniable, regardless of who created it or where it comes from. It's pure, distilled metamagic, offering a brief glimpse beyond the page and an assertion that characters have nothing to do with the pages they've been written into. Characters are separate; a soul vs. a body.

Immediately, I find myself compelled to head back over and give Snabe my thoughts, but before I get a chance to do so, another incantation pops into my head.

I smile, writing down the words and staring back at them as they stand proudly in beautiful black pixel. Another series of spell instructions comes, and then another, and another. Before I know it, I'm off and running, the words flowing freely from my hands in a way that I dare not second-guess or stop.

I've created plenty of spells, and I've mapped out components and movements and words, but this is something entirely different. This is something that I haven't felt in ages, Snabe's open expression pushing me to do some creative bleeding of my own.

I'm crafting my spell now.

By the time I come back up for air, it's late in the evening, only a sliver of sun left over the distant oceanic horizon. I've somehow blown through fifteen thousand words, a lot of crafting by any standard, and more than enough to send Minerma's way.

Once Minerma approves, I can start transferring this over to a magic parchment.

I'll talk to Snabe about his songspell in the morning, but right now, I'm exhausted.

STOLEN SPELLS

7

My eyes fly open in the darkness, woken with a start but unsure of why or how. My heart is pounding hard, a sign that my body is aware of something my brain is still struggling to understand.

I have no idea what time it is, but the splitting headache I'm experiencing after being ripped from my slumber makes me think it probably hasn't been too long. I was in a deep, deep sleep.

I remain completely still in bed, holding my breath as I listen intently to silence of my dark cabin.

Suddenly, a soft creek comes drifting out from the living room, followed but a quiet shuffling sound. I'm not sure if the noise is from my floorboards moving, or a squeaking chair by the kitchen table, but it's just barely more than you'd expect from a settling cabin.

Someone is in the house, I realize.

I reach over and grab my glasses from the bedside table, putting them on. I climb out of bed, looking for anything nearby that could possibly serve as protection. Unfortunately, there's little to choose from, but I do manage to find my wand in the darkness.

I hold it at the ready, prepared to manifest a simple yet powerful blast of raw magical energy.

Slowly, I creep towards the bedroom door, stopping right behind it and listening once more. There are no more creaks, but from here I can sense the air in the other rooms being moved is some way, gentle gusts rattling ever so slightly against the wooden door just inches from my head.

I realize now that my presence will be known the second I open this bedroom door, giving me little chance to sneak up on an intruder. My only option is to throw open the door and turn on the light, then pray that whoever's broken in is more akin to a raccoon than a robber.

Of course, the other option is to sit in here and quietly wait it out, but that's just not my style.

I take a deep breath and count down from ten, slowly preparing myself. I grip my wand tightly in my fist, ready for a powerful surge should the need arise.

When the countdown finally reaches zero, I throw open my bedroom door and flick on the light switch, casting the cabin in a brilliant yellow glow.

"Hey!" I shout out, hoping to startle my intruder, but then relaxing a bit when I realize nobody is here.

The cabin is completely empty.

Just to make sure, I spend the next few minutes peering behind couches and checking under tables, finding absolutely no concrete evidence of another presence. Despite the fact that nothing seems physically amiss, however, I still have a vague sense of unease gnawing away at me.

Eventually, I shut off all the lights and head back to bed, but not before checking on my cabin's front door. It's unlocked, something that should be frightening, but doesn't surprise me in the least. I've been having a lot of trouble with the rusted old bolt, and while this might be cause for alarm back in the big city where crime is rampant, there's not much to worry about out here.

At least, that used to be the case.

I double and triple check that the door is actually locked this time, then head back to bed, confident that this situation was nothing more than my mind playing tricks on me. I *have* been spellcrafting a lot, after all, and it's certainly caused my imagination to get fired up in the past.

This time, my departure from dreamland is much more pleasant, slowly coming to my senses as the afternoon light flickers gently across my eyelids. The curtains are drawn, but a single sliver of brilliant yellow has somehow snuck through.

I've slept in, making up for lost time after the curious events of last night.

Eventually, I manage to drag myself into an upright position, sitting with thick blankets pooled around me as I rub the sleep away from my eyes. I let out a long, satisfying yawn and then stretch my arms as far as they can possibly go, every muscle in my body pulled tight and then relaxing peacefully.

It's a good morning.

I climb out of bed and pull on my clothes, heading out to the kitchen for my morning cup of chocolate milk.

Warm light spills out across the cabin, making everything seem even cozier than usual.

I warm up the pot from last night and then pour myself a mug full, staring out at the ocean as I take a long, nourishing sip. Down below, Snabe's cabin is quiet and peaceful, and although it's probably already noon, I'm guessing the dinosaur is sleeping in after a long night. After our rendezvous in the woods, I wouldn't be surprised if he was just as inspired as I was.

Excited by the incantations I'm getting down, I'd like to jump back in to my crafting as quickly as possible, but I also know that my creative brain is never where it should be this soon after waking up. Instead, I opt to take a stroll down to the beach, soaking in some of this rare sun and allowing the fresh ocean breeze to tickle my skin. When I return, I'll get back to work.

Maybe I can even move from the computer to an actual magical parchment.

Grabbing a coat and toting along my mug of chocolate milk, I head out the door and make my way down to towards the beach.

Lately, I've been collecting sea glass that washes up on the shore, a beautiful phenomenon that always makes me chuckle over the sheer irony of how it comes to be. People always see this multicolored glass, worn down into soft, round shapes, as a natural part of the coastline, but that couldn't be farther from the truth.

Sea glass is created when beach going partiers throw their empty bottles out into the water, or crack them open over rocks in a drunken stupor. The tide inevitably comes in and sweeps these dangerous shards out into the ocean, turning them over and over again in the tides for days, months, or even years. Eventually, these pieces will return to the shore in the form of gorgeous, tumbled glass, literal trash that's been refined into something extraordinary. All that it took was a little time and a little patience, scraping away at the rough edges until, eventually; all that's left is the shimmering beauty within.

When I reach the beach, I immediately get to work strolling along the water's edge, my head down and my focus locked intently onto the pebbles and sand that pass beneath my feet. It's not long before I find a striking blue piece of sea glass, larger than most and perfectly rounded on the edges to create a strange sort of oval. I lift it up and gaze directly through it, smiling at the way it casts the whole world in a cool, pleasant hue.

Suddenly, I stop, noticing through the glass that Snabe is standing stoically on the hill above me. I wave, but he doesn't smile with he sees me. Instead, the muscular parasaurolophus begins marching down the stairs before him.

"Hey! I have *so* much to talk to you about!" I call out, strolling over to meet the dinosaur halfway.

It's only then I detect just how serious Snabe's expression remains. Something is definitely wrong.

"How could you do that to me?" Snabe demands to know, stopping abruptly.

I furrow my brow in confusion. "Do what? What are you even talking about?"

"You know *exactly* what I'm talking about," Snabe continues, simmering with anger. "The songspell."

"I *loved* the songspell!" I gush. "That's what I wanted to tell you. It's incredible!"

"That was for your ears only, Harriet," Snabe reminds me. "You knew that. I told you to keep it a secret!"

"I did!" I cry out, completely taken off guard by this bizarre situation. "I listened to it once last night and that was it. Who the hell would I share it with?"

"Everyone?" Snabe blurts. "The whole fucking world?"

I shake my head. "I have no idea what you're talking about."

"The songspell leaked last night," Snabe informs me. "It's the first thing anyone's seen of Seven Inch Nails in years, and now it's on every wizarding blog."

"Well… that's a good thing, isn't it?" I stammer.

"Not if it's unfinished!" Snabe yells. "That could have been a massive spell, it could have altered the fabric of meta reality forever! It's the most important songspell I've ever written, and now it's out in the world as a half-baked nightmare."

"I don't know what to tell you," I finally offer, shaking my head. "I didn't send it to any wizarding blogs."

Snabe just stares at me blankly, his silence saying more than words ever could.

"Harriet, is there anything you want to tell me?" he finally asks, the intensity behind his eyes not letting up for a second.

"I don't know what you want me to say," I stammer.

"You were the only one with a copy of that track," Snabe informs me. "I gave you a drive yesterday, and now it's all over the internet this morning? How *do you* think I should react to this? There's only one version of this song with vocal incantations on it, and I sure as hell didn't send it out myself."

"Well, neither did I," I tell him, slowly shifting away from my defensive stance. I'm getting frustrated now, and although I feel for Snabe in this terrible situation, there's nothing I can do if the dinosaur refuses to believe me.

"That songspell was my last chance of getting back into the spotlight," Snabe states bluntly, a crushing emotional weight to his tone. "The magic schools loved it, my manager loved it… you loved it. Now everything is completely fucked."

"I'm sorry," is all that I can offer.

Snabe shakes his head. "Why did you do it, Harriet?" he questions. "So you could tell the world about how you fucked over the great Snabe Rezmor during your next wizarding talk? Or was it to get back at me for not sending Dellatrix home?"

Suddenly, my blood runs cold. My thoughts immediately drift back to last night, to the possible intruder that may or may not have been sneaking around in my cabin. This morning, the thumb drive was still exactly where I left it, but that doesn't mean Dellatrix couldn't have made a copy for herself.

"Oh my god," I blurt. "I thought I heard someone in my cabin last night."

"What does that have to do with anything?" Snabe questions, frustrated.

"Dellatrix must have stolen the file," I reply, my eyes going wide.

Snabe takes a deep breath, struggling to remain calm. "Is that really how you're going to play this?"

My eyes narrow, finally losing it completely. "What the hell is wrong with you? Do you not see how terrible that motorcycle is? She's manipulative and evil, and for some reason you just completely ignore it."

Snabe doesn't deny this, but he defends her anyway. "Don't try and pass this onto someone else just because you're jealous," the dinosaur tells me with a smirk, the arrogant jerk that I once knew now bubbling back up to the surface.

"Having anything to do with you was as huge mistake," I snap, seething with anger. "I thought you could grow, I thought you could overcome whatever made you into this monster, but I was dead wrong."

Snabe grins and then shrugs. "Well, it's a good thing I don't get a damn about what you think," he tells me, then turns around and starts heading back up towards his cabin. "Let's never talk again!" the parasaurolophus yells back over his shoulder. "Good? Good."

I take a deep breath as I watch him go, I mired of emotions flowing through my body in rapid succession. The anger quickly transforms into sadness, a great wave of melancholy washing over me when I realize that things will never be the same.

The longer I sit with this, however, the more I realize that it's probably for the better. I can't change Snabe if he's not willing to change himself, and as long as he's unwilling to let go of this bad boy lifestyle, he's always going to find a way to return to his asshole roots. Snabe is a piece of glass that simply refuses to be polished by the currents; sharp, dangerous, and when it comes right down to it, obnoxiously brittle.

I should've known better, and eventually this anger turns around to point directly at myself. What the hell was I thinking?

Wanting nothing more than to be safely behind the glowing screen of my word processor, I begin to make my way back up the hill. I stop when I reach the dock, however, noticing something strange out of the corner of my eye. A long wooden paddle has been wedged under the structure, just barely poking out from the dock's edge. It's too far up the beach to be swept away by any currents, just barely above the water line during even the highest tides.

Curious, I walk over and pull out the oar, looking it over. This belongs to a nearby dingy, old and unused as it sits overturned on the opposite end of the beach. There's no reason for this paddle to be all the way over here.

The second that I turn this oar over in my hands I gasp aloud, my eyes focused on the large circle of rust colored blood that has dried across its wooden blade. A long blond hair is caught between a crack in the wood, hanging limply.

It's easy to extrapolate what happened down here on the night Dellatrix ended up in the hospital. Of course, the timing was always suspicious, but now everything adds up completely. Dellatrix didn't slip and fall on the dock, she hit herself in the face with an oar. It's also possible that Braco did it for her, but regardless of how this occurred, Dellatrix wasn't unconscious when she hit the water. The whole thing was just a ploy to gain back some attention and sympathy from Snabe, and the whole thing worked like a charm.

Of course, the type of person who would intentionally send themselves to the hospital would also have no problem breaking into a cabin and copying a computer file. They also wouldn't think twice about sending that file out to every magic school and wizarding publication they could find, potentially destroying a bard's album launch and long awaited career comeback just to frame someone else.

Snabe is certainly angry right now, but he's not dumb. I could bring this paddle right up to his door and blow the lid off of everything.

But I refuse.

If Snabe's going to grow up, then he needs to do it for himself. There's already enough evidence that Dellatrix is utterly insane, but Snabe absolutely refuses to give up on his bad boy lifestyle and the motorcycles who come with it. These are his choices to make, and if I force his hand, then it's never going to stick.

Let's be honest, it probably won't ever stick regardless. The dinosaur is a lost cause.

I drag the oar over to the ocean's edge, then pull it back behind me. With one powerful movement, I swing the paddle forward and toss it as far as I can into the ocean, letting go of any attachment I'd felt myself developing to this arrogant, but fascinating, parasaurolophus spellcrafter.

The oar was constructed to float, so it remains buoyant upon on the surface. It doesn't drift back towards me, however. Instead, the paddle begins to make its way out into the ocean, pulled away by the currents as it begins its journey. It could end up anywhere now, tumbling around in the island currents for years, or heading out into the middle of the Atlantic.

It's kind of exciting to think about.

HARRIET METAMALIUM

8

Islands, by their very nature, have a way of trapping you. There's an edge on every side, a border that's more than just a thin line on a map. Even when you're ready to leave, an entire process must be undertaken to bring that desire into reality.

I've been considering it.

The thing is, I'm not ready to leave, not just yet. This place has been too inspiring for me to throw it all away and start over again. Especially given the way that my spell publishers are reacting to the first draft of this powerful ritual.

"They love it," Minerma tells me, her voice overflowing with excitement as it tumbles out through my phone and across my ears.

I'm sitting on a bench in the middle of town, surrounded by business that are closed for the season. It's peaceful, like an imaginary universe where I'm the only one left on Earth. The only sound is Minerma's excited chatter through my phone and the soft ring of the flagpole nearby, rustling in the breeze while a metallic portion of the rope taps over and over again against its hollow tube.

I brought along my wand, and at this point I wave it through the air above me. *"Musicus localium,"* I murmur quietly, manifesting a pleasant tune to fill in some of that auditory space.

It suddenly hits me that this was originally a bard spell, and I try my best to push this notion away as quickly as it arrives.

Fuck bard spells.

This is where I go to work now, far from the cabin that once felt so warm and cozy but now provides nothing but miserable memories and a close proximity to the one dinosaur I'd rather not be around.

"That's good to hear," I tell Minerma. "I love it, too."

"Seriously, though," my spellcraft agent continues gushing. "The first spell was fantastic, it really was, but this is a whole over level. Everything is so raw and real and… ambitious. You're really stretching your limits with this."

"Thank you," I reply, not knowing what else to say.

My agent lowers her voice again. "Is this actually going to work? A spell that brings you the one thing you need, exactly when you need it? It feels very abstract."

"It'll work once I get all the kinks out," I offer assumingly, trying to put all of the failed casting attempts out of my mind. I'm beginning to think I've bitten off a little more than I can chew with this one. I might not even be halfway done, but I don't say this.

"When can we get the actual parchment?" Minerma questions. "The wizards over here are excited to try casting it for themselves."

I stare at the empty shop windows across the street from me, my mind drifting away as I consider what it must be like to live here in the summer time. I'm trying to avoid my agent's question, because I'm not entirely sure of the answer.

"Hello?" Minerma finally blurts. "Did I lose you."

"I'm sorry," I stammer, pulled back into myself.

"When can we get the final ritual on parchment?" Minerma repeats.

I hesitate for a moment. "Am I talking to you as a spellcraft agent, or as a friend?" I question.

"Both," she informs me. "Always both."

"I don't think that's gonna cut it," I laugh. "Can you tell the agent to step outside?"

Minerma pauses. "Of course," she finally replies, a surprisingly understanding move for sure a tight-laced woman. "What's up?"

"It was all flowing," I tell her, "I was writing incantation after incantation of really incredible stuff. Magic I could be proud of. I was in my groove, but now there's nothing. I'm back to square one."

"What are you saying, exactly?" Minerma continues.

"I saying I don't know when you'll get the parchment," I confess. "I've got a lot of stuff to sort out before my mind is ready for that. This spell is great, but it reminds me of a place that I'd rather not think about right now."

Minerma lets out a long sigh. "You fucked him, didn't you?" she finally questions, stepping outside of her strict professionalism for a moment. I think this is the first time I've ever heard Minerma swear, and it completely throws me for a loop.

"What?" I blurt defensively, then immediately realize I've been caught. "Yeah. How'd you know?"

"I mean, Snabe has a certain powerful charm," Minerma states bluntly.

"Don't remind me," I groan.

"So, what happened?" Minerma continues. "You thought you could change the bad boy bard, but now you realize the dinosaur's a lost cause and you've been wasting your time?"

"I think I knew that from the beginning," I admit. "I just hoped I was wrong."

"Well, that *does* explain why this spell is so… I don't know. Angsty?" continues Minerma.

"If you met these motorcycles, you'd be angsty, too," I reply.

Minerma considers my words for a moment, trying to make sense of it all. "With all this drama, I'm confused why the crafting stopped," my agent admits. "I thought that's what got you going in the first place."

"It was," I admit. "I just don't want to be in that place anymore. I don't want to be around those people. I don't want to see… him."

"Ah, sweetheart," Minerma sighs, her tone changing to one of genuine sympathy. "That dinosaur really did a number on you, didn't he?"

"I think so," I confirm with a laugh.

"Well, what do you need?" my agent questions, getting down to business. "How are we going to keep things moving? Because what you've got so far is incredible. I don't care what it takes; this spell cannot stop moving forward."

"I need my advance," I finally tell her. "I know that it's supposed to come after I've turned in my first parchment draft, but if I'm ever gonna get there, then I can't be staying in your cabin any longer."

Minerma lets these words linger in the air between us for a moment, trying to piece together a plan in her head. "I think I can work something out," my agent finally says, "but only because the magic you've sent us is so fucking amazing. You keep turning in ideas like this and you'll be able to do whatever you want."

I let out a long sigh of relief. "Thank you," I gush. "That's such a relief."

"I'll get the money carried over to your account by giant owls as soon as possible," Minerma assures me.

"Wait, really?" I stammer.

"No, I'm just kidding. We use wire transfer," Minerma offers. "Now get back to work."

I tried to find a place on the opposite end of the island, I really did, but for some reason nothing seemed to suit me. The original cabin was so cozy, so perfect for a wizard like myself, that some random shack up for seasonal rental just won't do.

Of course, I'm also working with a limited budget, and although the advance for my second spell was quite generous, it needs to last me a long time, maybe even several years. Besides, I haven't even gotten half of the way through writing this one.

Fortunately, I eventually found a place that called out to me in the same way Minerma's cabin did, a small cottage nestled up in the woods that overlooks the same cove I was originally trapped in. I was weary about being this close to Snabe's place, partly out of my disdain for the parasaurolophus, partly because I'd rather Dellatrix didn't know where I lived. After the break in, there's no telling what that motorcycle is capable of, but I'm also trying to deny her any sway over my life at this point, for better or worse.

The cottage has a deck that's absolutely perfect for spellcraft on, allowing me to sit out in the shade of the massive evergreens while I gaze down at the sparkling water far, far below. It's *technically* possible to hike down to the beach from here, but even with *treemus passious* it would take a very, very long time and you might end up breaking your legs when you tumble down over the steep, rocky cliff side.

I feel protected here, perched up high so I can see the rest of the world coming. The only thing this private getaway hasn't provided yet, however, are words on the parchment.

The move was quick and easy, but now that I'm here, the inspiration I assumed would come bubbling back has refused to rear its head. Instead, I find myself staring at my spell parchment, then hopping back on the word processor for hours on end, then switching over to Solitaire, wasting away my day as digital playing cards dance their way across my laptop computer screen.

Lately, I've started confronting an utterly terrifying thought, something that has been hinted at by a number of wizards, including myself, but rarely ever said out loud.

Is it possible I can't create without pain in my life? Is drama the fuel that I need to survive as a wizard?

I certainly hope not, but the longer I sit up here on my perch, slowly burning through my spell advance money as the days stretch into weeks, I'm not so sure anymore. The most productive I've been during this entire trip was when things were getting the craziest.

Back then, ritual incantations were flowing like water from my fingertips.

I've tried everything to get myself started up again, struggling to jump my creative motor through long walks in the woods and one or two day trips to the other islands nearby. Nothing seems to help, although there was one day I found myself strolling closer and closer to the old cabin, tempting fate with every step as I imagined that brilliant yellow sports car rumbling around the corner.

The car never came, but that was the one of the few nights I actually managed to get some ink down on the parchment.

I've also become a regular at Captain Orion's Cove, showing up like clockwork every Wednesday and Friday night for dinner.

The waitress, Gobby, has made a personal promise that she'll warn me if she ever spots Snabe coming, but he never does. She's good about not taking sides, and although she clearly loves the guy, it's quite apparent to her that I've got good reasons for steering clear.

Tonight is Friday night, and I'm excited to be getting out of the house for a bit. I've been staring at my computer screen and a shelf full of spell components all day, struggling to coax forth the words that refuse to come. It's exhausting, the mental drain causing me to physically ache after hours and hours of absolutely no progress.

But now I'm out of there, on the road towards town with the windows down as the cool wind whips itself refreshingly across my face. I'm blasting music, letting myself get swept away in the sound as my phone shuffles through every hit I've got.

Classic after classic comes spilling through my car speakers, sing-along jams that have me raising my voice and pushing the speed limit. It's only when an old Seven Inch Nails track arrives that my breath catches in my throat.

It's their first hit, an up-tempo rock and roll spell that blasts along with hooky, sloppy, rock and roll brilliance.

This metamagic spell creates swirling, magical text in the air that describes what's going on in the listeners field of vision. It's a simple trick, but the beauty of this glowing neon writing is something to be admired.

Of course, my first instinct is to reach out and turn the stereo off, but as my hand flies in that direction I stop myself. Now I'm listening intently, my fingers hovering over the nob but refusing to change the volume.

The words, "hovering over the nob but refusing the change the volume" appear on the side of the road next to me, swaying from side to side as I drive past.

I'm not gonna lie, this is a really good songspell, and one that I haven't heard in ages.

If this had happened two months back I'd be thrilled to sing along, but now I'm not quite sure how I feel while Snabe's vocal incantations cascade across my ears. I'm flooded by a potent mixture of emotions, from disgust, to anger, to a strange and powerful joy. The connection between Snabe and I had been so strong in such a short amount of time, and a small taste of that feeling once more is wonderful.

It's also sad.

I reach out and take the volume knob in my hand, intending to turn it down but then shifting directions at the last minute. Instead, I crank up the volume, giving in to the spell as it flows across me, singing along like my life depends on it. I'm belting at the top of my lungs, letting out all the anger and frustration that's been pent up inside of me.

The words "I'm belting at the top of my lungs, letting out all the anger and frustration that's been pent up inside of me," appear above the road as I cruise under them, sizzling with colorful, dancing light.

When the songspell finally finishes, I fall back into my driver's seat, exhausted.

Snabe is still an insufferable asshole, but that felt nice.

It's not long before I pull into the parking lot of Captain Orion's Cove, turning off my engine and climbing out of the car. My mouth is already watering as the powerful scent of the restaurant wafts out into the parking lot, a familiar hint of the incredible meal that's about to follow. If there were ever a time for the term *hidden gem*, Captain Orion's Cove would be it.

I walk down the path and open the door, immediately greeted by Gobby.

"Hey!" I cry with a wide smile and open arms, giving the woman a strong hug. "How's it going tonight?"

I release my grip and then glance around the room, staring in shock at the empty tables before me. The place is utterly vacant, which is routine during the afternoon but absolutely unheard of on a Friday night.

The next strange thing I notice is that a corner of the restaurant has been cleared out, the tables missing but a small stool and microphone set up in their place. Speakers are situated on either side of them.

Behind, a keyboard and acoustic guitar are positioned, as well as a large upright bass that's been left leaning up against the wall.

"We're trying out an open mic," Gobby informs me.

I laugh. "I hate to be the bearer of bad news, but it's not going well."

Gobby smiles and leads me over to my usual table, sitting me down and offering a menu. I wave her away. "Just the usual," I say.

The woman nods, then turns and heads back towards the kitchen, disappearing through the swinging doorway.

I gaze out at the ocean view through the window before me, taken aback by just how much it reminds me of the date that me and Snabe once had here, not so long ago. Tonight's massive yellow moon is reflecting off of the water in exactly the same way, shimmering and dancing over the waves in a way that is almost hypnotizing.

Between this moment of reflection and the Seven Inch Nails song on my way here, I actually find myself missing Snabe.

Of course, I often reminisce on the bountiful inspiration that his drama seemed to bring me, but this new, warm nostalgia for the dinosaur is not that at all. The kind of yearning I feel is simple, without any cues from my lacking creativity or stagnant writing.

I just miss him.

Not that it really matters. The guy's a mess and, without significant personal changes, he's awful for me to be around. I can't get involved with someone like that, I just can't.

Snabe needs to fix some important aspects of his bad boy personality before I ever see him again. I can't be the one to do it.

My thoughts are suddenly interrupted by someone clearing their throat over the microphone, their rattle echoing out loudly across the empty restaurant. I turn my head and stop abruptly, utterly stunned by the sight of Snabe sitting perched atop his stool with an acoustic guitar cradled in his arms. He's wearing a dark button up shirt that's been rolled up past his elbows, revealing colorful, muscular forearms that are completely covered in scales and tattoos.

Immediately, a number of different emotions swim through me, some of them good and some of them bad. Still, I remain seated.

Snabe and me lock eyes, but he doesn't give me his typical self-assured smirk. Rather, the parasaurolophus nods, as though in reverence of the fact that I'm still in my seat instead of bolting for the door.

"Hello everyone," Snabe finally says into the microphone, waving to a crowd that's not actually there. "Welcome to the first Captain Orion's Cove open mic night. We have one performer this evening… yours truly."

Seconds later, Gobby emerges from the kitchen with a sizzling plate of my usual order, the cod spaghetti. It's only been a minute or so since I sat down, so it's clear now that my food was prepared early.

"You promised you'd tell me if Snabe was on his way in," I whisper to Gobby out of the corner of my mouth.

The woman nods empathically, but not *too* empathically. "I never said anything about telling you he was already here."

I roll my eyes as Gobby leaves, offering a faint smile. Whatever Snabe's trying to do here tonight, she's not responsible. I can't hold this against her.

"It's weird," Snabe continues. "As a bad boy, this is the point in the story where I made a huge gesture to win you back. I know you'll appreciate it, but I'm still super nervous in front of you."

The dinosaur's admission makes me immediately crack a smile, unable to contain myself.

"This song is for a very special woman," Snabe says proudly. "Someone I didn't appreciate when we first met, because I'm written to be a toxic jerk. At this point, she doesn't owe me anything, and that's not why I'm here. I just wanted her to hear this spell because there was once a time when she really, really liked it. I've been working on this spell for a long time, but I think it's finally finished."

Snabe takes a deep, muffled breath into the microphone. Moments later, the muscular parasaurolophus's claws start to move, his right hand strumming gently as he begins to play the first beautiful chords the gorgeous acoustic number that I know and love.

"This spell is called *Harriet Metamalium"* Snabe offers.

What follows is one of the most incredible bardic spell performances I've ever seen. Snabe is completely in sync with the music, his body swaying gently from side to side on the stool as he croons away. The playing is loose and emotive, but not so much that it takes away from the dinosaur's performance. I can tell that he's been rehearsing, perfectly aware of every tiny moment that he creates.

The magical effects of this songspell quickly begin to take hold, even more refined than they were the last time I heard it. Not only do I see myself as a character on a page, I see the actual words themselves. I gaze out through the limits of this world and see the reader themselves, their mouths instinctively curling up into a smile when they realize they're being referenced.

Most importantly, I realize this body is something the author places characters into, but it's not the character themselves. Characters can jump from story to story, whether it's a young adult fantasy or an explicit romance parody, and still maintain the things that make them so special and unique and important. They can be placed into a body that fits them perfectly, or one that is hopelessly out of sync; a professor, a rock star, or a dinosaur.

Either way, what makes them who they are is the heart and soul of each character, not the shell that it's wrapped in.

As I listen, it's hard to keep the tears from welling up in my eyes and fogging up my glasses. I'm still upset with Snabe, but the raw emotion being projected across this room is simply too much for me to maintain my composure. We're communicating without speaking now, the lyrics and melody saying endlessly more than any conversation ever could.

When Snabe finishes, I quickly wipe the tears away from my eyes, offering up my solo applause that fills the room awkwardly.

"Thanks, that's my set," Snabe says into the microphone. "I'd love to play a little more but I've got dinner plans. Don't worry though, Celly, Dodwyn and Borcan are gonna set the mood for everyone now."

Three figures make their way out of the kitchen as Snabe leaves his stool. They take their positions at every instrument, quickly setting themselves up before breaking out into a pleasant, romantic jazz tune.

Snabe strolls up to the table, standing for a moment and taking me in. "First, I'm sorry," the dinosaur finally says.

I nod. "Apology not accepted," I inform him. "Yet."

"Can I sit down?" Snabe asks.

I pretend to think about his request for a minute, then finally reply. "Sure."

Snabe sits in the chair directly across from me.

Moments later Gobby appears with a rare steak, placing it before the bard. "Enjoy your meal," Gobby offers, smiling and making direct eye contact with me to see if I'm okay.

I give Gobby a thankful nod before she turns and leaves.

"I'm sure you've got a lot to say," I finally start in, "but before you tell me anything I just have to ask, why do I recognize the guys in this band?"

Snabe seems confused at first, then glances back over his shoulder in a moment of understanding. "Oh yeah, I bet you do," the parasaurolophus replies with a chuckle. "I met Dodwyn and Borcan on our first date here. Had to kick their asses for being obnoxious and drunk, but we're cool now. They're actually great guys, just had a bit of a problem. Two weeks sober now for each of them. It's a start."

I shake my head in amazement. "You just… became friends with them?"

Snabe nods. "I saw the guys in town a little while after our fight and we started talking. Turns out they're pretty damn good players. They've been recording with me. Borcan is Celly's husband, actually."

"That's… pretty wild," is all that I can say, then backtrack a bit. "Are you sober, too? Off the chocolate milk?"

"For now," Snabe replies with a smile. "I'm trying."

That smile. Of all the things I'd missed about this dinosaur, I'd forgotten about how intoxicatingly charming his sharp toothed smile was. Despite the hardness of his bad boy romance archetype exterior, this simple but fleeting expression is like a window into the soul of the sweet, innocent boy that once was.

The second I feel his charisma creeping its way through my veins, however, I immediately put up my defenses. The spell was nice, but there's more going on here than just a simple misunderstanding.

"I have to tell you this up front," I begin. "I'm not gonna be with you if you've got those motorcycles hanging around."

"I know that," Snabe tells me with understanding grace. "They're gone."

I'm completely blindsided by the bard's words, taken aback but this unexpected revelation. "Are you serious?" I question.

Snabe nods. "I sent them back to work for Magrid at Bogmorts again. They used to drive him around. Well, I sent Dellatrix at least. I know she's the one who leaked the spellsong to those wizard blogs."

"How did you find out?" I ask him.

Snabe shrugs. "It was obvious from the beginning, I just didn't want to see it. That's not why I kicked her out though, I kicked her out because she's not you."

"Not even close," I affirm.

Snabe laughs. "Braco's still on the island somewhere, though. Full disclosure."

I raise my eyebrows.

"It's not like that," Snabe assures me. "She's getting off the chocolate milk, too. I set her up with a cabin on the other side."

While I'd rather Braco was just completely removed from Snabe's life, there's something about the care that Snabe has given her situation that's actually kind of sweet. *She* was never really the problem anyway, seemingly swept away by Dellatrix's influence and too weak to do anything about it.

"So, it's just you now," I reply, mulling this revelation over in my head.

The bad boy dinosaur nods.

"How's the recording going?" I question. "Getting those hit bard spells tracked?"

The handsome parasaurolophus takes a deep breath into his broad chest. "Well, that session band is great," he says, nodding over towards the guys as they continue to serenade us with beautiful, sweeping jazz chords. "But honestly, I'm having a little trouble again."

My eyes light up as the dinosaur says this. It's not that I want him to struggle, far from it, but there's a truth in his admission that I find myself deeply relating to.

"Don't get too excited," Snabe laughs.

I shake my head. "I'm sorry, it's just… I can't get anything done, either. When everything was going down between us, I was completely on fire. The rituals were flowing like never before. Now, I feel like I'm right back where I started."

"Me too," Snabe admits, then changes his expression to one of grave concern. "You know that's not why I'm here, right."

"I know," I reply with a laugh. "I don't need that drama in my life, anyway. Being inspired is great, but if that's what it takes to fuel my creative side, I'd rather just get a job as a finance wizard or something."

"What if it's not the drama that inspires us?" Snabe continues.

I consider this. "What else would it be?"

Snabe declines to reply, staring out the window for a moment and then shrugging it off. "That's not why I'm here," he repeats, almost to himself. "I'm here for you."

Hearing the bard say this so directly once again fills my body with fluttering butterflies, only this time I decline to push them away. Instead, I give in to the powerful longing, letting it sweep over me like a powerful wave from the nearby ocean. It feels good to accept the potent current that I've been struggling against for so long, but I'm happy I resisted this long.

Giving Snabe another chance would've meant nothing if he was the same dinosaur from our last encounter, an endless cycle through bad boy behavior and the eventual destruction of our relationship before it even had a chance to form. Sure, that still might happen, and I'll take every step forward with a massive heap of skepticism, but I believe the parasaurolophus when he tells me that he's grown.

He's done more than just tell me, in fact. He's shown me.

I suddenly realize what Snabe was about to say, offering up the words myself. "What if it's not the drama and destruction that inspires us?" I suggest. "What if we're inspired by each other?"

"Exactly," Snabe replies with a smile. "I mean, that's not why I'm here. I'd give up the magic completely if it meant spending another day with you."

"I wouldn't ask you to," I counter. "I like your spells."

"And I like your spells," Snabe replies.

I burst out laughing. "You haven't even read my spells!"

Snabe reaches into the breast pocket of his jacket and pulls out a small, travel-sized scroll of *Bubblus Morphus*. "I got it online," the man informs me. "I'm not great at performing it yet, but I'm getting there. I made one bubble."

I smile. "Well, I appreciate the effort."

"Kinda sad sounding incantation for a hot-to-trot spell, though," Snabe continues.

I nod. "Well, it was written during a sad time in my life."

Snabe hesitates, trying to choose his words carefully before continuing with whatever he's about to say. I have to admit, seeing him do this is even more charming than I expected, a complete shift from the dinosaur who used to run his mouth and say whatever he'd like without any regard for the consequences. I'm certain this isn't a habit that's been eliminated completely, but the fact that he's taking special care for me is deeply impressive.

"I don't think you need to be sad to spellcraft," he says. "I think you can be happy and fulfilled and healthy... and your new spell will be just as good."

"Why do you think that?" I question.

"Because that's how I feel about *my* spells now," Snabe explains. "It just took meeting you for me to realize it."

I want to believe Snabe so badly, but there's still a kernel of doubt hidden in the back of my mind. The tortured bard is a stereotype that's been around since the beginning of art itself. So many of the greatest creators, whether a painter, a musician, or a wizard like myself, have felt like tortured souls.

There's something dangerous about it, sexy even, and it's ingrained in our bones.

But that's no way to live, and the chance to prove an age old idea wrong is more than a little exciting, especially if I get to do it with Snabe by my side.

"This is really nice," I tell the dinosaur across from me. "Let's appreciate it for a moment."

We spend the next while eating and enjoying the music, reliving our first date and then eventually discussing other dates we'd like to have in the future. I give in to his charms completely, and by the time we're finished with our food, Snabe and me are completely on the same page.

"So the songspell is finished," I observe. "It's really beautiful."

"It's *almost* done," Snabe informs me. "Very close. It's effecting characters within the book, but I want it to do more than that. I want the *reader* to know they're beautiful and strong and important in whatever body they inhabit."

"I'm sorry it leaked online," I offer. "I can't believe Dellatrix would do that just to fuck with me."

Snabe takes a deep breath. "It's my fault for keeping the motorcycle so close when there were so many warning signs. I can't blame anyone but myself. Then again, where would the conflict in the third act be?"

I shake my head. "It's weird hearing you talk like this," I admit. "You really have changed a lot."

"Well, I met a very strong woman who wasn't going to wait around while I stayed stuck in my rut," Snabe continues. "That's not to say I'll never make another mistake. In fact, I'll probably make a lot, but I'm gonna give it my best shot."

"That's good to hear," I reply, reaching across the table and running my fingertips over Snabe's large claws.

"The spell leak was a blessing in disguise, actually," Snabe informs me. "The track went viral. Everyone's clamoring to hear the final songspell."

"Really?" I blurt, my eyes going wide. "That's great! Why haven't you finished it yet?"

"I still have one more thing I'd like to record," he tells me. "Have you ever sung backup vocals?"

It's weird being back here at the cabin, looking up at the dark cottage and the beautiful star filled sky above it. I honestly never thought I'd return to this cove after gathering my things and heading up into the hills.

Snabe pulls out his keys and unlocks the door. He starts to push it open but I stop him.

"Wait," I suddenly blurt.

Snabe turns to me with a look of deep concern. "What is it?"

"I just realized that I've never been inside your place before," I tell him. "I have this whole idea in my head of what it looks like, and that's about to go away forever."

"Whatever you're imagining is probably much more exciting than the real thing, so savor it," Snabe replies with a smile.

The man pushes open the door of his cabin and flips on the light, revealing an immaculately clean-living space with beautiful, ultra-modern furnishings. It's gorgeous, but not cozy, with a colors scheme leaning heavily towards green and grey.

Hanging on the wall are banners from his old fraternity at bardic college, emblazoned with the symbol of a lizard.

"Did you bring in all this furniture yourself?" I question, stepping inside.

Snabe nods. "I had someone do it for me, but I helped pick out a lot of the stuff from my old magic frat back in college, *Lizardin*. That's why I'm a parasaurolophus in this book, get it?"

I shake my head. "Not really. Half the time I have no idea what you metamagic wizards are talking about."

Snabe decides to change the subject. "You like the place?"

"I prefer the rustic cottage feeling," I admit, "but this suits you."

I stroll over to the stainless-steel fridge, opening it up and checking out the contents. Instead of the decaying leftovers and various condiments that I'd expect from a bachelor parasaurolophus like Snabe, I find an entire shelf of bottled water, along with a vast assortment of fresh fruits and vegetables.

"Wow, you really *have* been working on yourself," I admit, "and it's so clean in here."

"It wasn't before," Snabe admits with a laugh.

The hulking, muscular dinosaur leads me through his small living room to a door that, I assume, once lead to a bedroom. Instead, the original door has been replaced by one that is thick and heavy, a small window built into the middle so that you can see between. A computer and mixing board covering in magical, bardic runes are set up nearby, while two large speakers hang on either side of the doorway, completing the makeshift recording booth.

"Aw, so these are the culprits," I laugh, strolling over and running my fingers along the hard grid of the speaker grill.

Snabe winces a bit. "Yeah. Sorry about that."

"I'll consider forgiving you," I tell him with a smile. "I've still got a lot of apologies to consider though, so that's going on the bottom of the pile."

"Fair enough," the dinosaur concedes.

"So this is where it all happens," I continue.

Snabe nods. "Are you ready to get in there and sing some incantations?"

A wave of anxiety suddenly rushes over me. When I accepted Snabe's offer back at the restaurant, I hadn't quite considered what it would actually feel like to sit here with him in the studio. When you take all the complexities of our relationship out of the equation, he's still a bardic legend, a man whose voice I spent years listening to and admiring. The prospect of performing any kind of serious spellcraft in front of him is absolutely terrifying, let alone *bardic* spellcraft.

I normally have no problem stepping up to conquer the various situations that arise before me. I'm a badass, and proud of it. For some reason, however, this moment perfectly strikes upon my deepest insecurities.

It's not that I have a terrible signing voice, either. I can carry a tune, and nobody's ever complained after hearing me rip it up for a karaoke night, or belt out Happy Birthday. I'm just not sure if I have any business being immortalized forever on an actual album track from a talented, well known bard. Wizards create their spells in a very different way, pouring over spell books and experimenting with various components for days on end.

It's nothing like this.

Snabe notices my hesitation. "You'll be fine," he promises.

"You sure about that?" I question. "Because I get the feeling I'm going to deeply embarrass myself."

Snabe laughs. "I guess we're both feeling a little out of character tonight," he says. "You'll be great. If you don't like the way it sounds in the track, then we'll just delete it right away and nobody will ever hear your part. Fair?"

This is just barely enough to get me into the vocal booth.

Snabe leads me into the converted bedroom and places me before a large, beautifully crafted orb of swirling magical energy that acts as some kind of microphone. There are amplifiers and guitars everywhere in here, as well as a massive drum kit positioned in the corner. Snabe hands me a set of headphones.

"Put these on," he instructs me. "The chorus incantation is one word and it's your name, so I think you'll be fine on the lyrics."

I slip on my headphones and stand up straight, watching as Snabe leaves the room and closes the door tightly behind him. He walks over to the computer and presses a few keys, then moments later the sound of my own voice miraculously appears within my headphones. It sounds like I'm in a large, spacious room now, my voice echoing out off of the invisible walls.

"This is weird," I announce, taking note of the cascading sound of my voice through this swirling orb.

"You'll get used to it once the track starts," Snabe assures me, his voice suddenly appearing within my headphones. It sounds as though he's standing right over my shoulder.

"Sounds good," I reply, taking a deep breath.

"I'll start the song and you can just listen for a bit. When it gets to the chorus, all you have to do is sing the same thing that's already there," my new producer explains. "Think you've got that?"

"I think so," I confirm.

"You ready?" Snabe asks one last time.

I don't respond.

"Harriet?" he questions.

I let out all the air from my lungs in a long sigh, trying to collect my thoughts. "I have no idea why I'm so nervous," I finally admit. "This isn't like me."

"That's okay," the dinosaur offers. "I've been doing this my whole life, so it's easy for me. Even the most talented wizards have trouble their first time working on bard spells. You've got nothing to worry about."

"Okay," I finally say with a nod, as though confirming this with both Snabe, and myself. "Roll it."

Seconds later, the songspell begins to play through my headphones, soft and sweet as it drifts past my ears. I'm immediately taken by just how beautiful this recorded version is, much cleaner than the demo Snabe had presented me some time ago. It sounds like a light piano has been added in the background, which just serves to elevate things even more.

I begin to see the metareality of our existence opening up before me, but I try my best to rein in my attention and remain present in *this* story.

The chorus finally arrives and I open my mouth to sing, but nothing comes out.

Snabe lets the song play on a little bit longer and then stops the track.

"I'm sorry," I tell him. "I just… I don't know if I can do this. I'm not a bard."

"Fair enough," Snabe continues. "You want to stop?"

His words are a relief, but I hesitate to accept them. I've never been one to give up easily, and I do appreciate this opportunity of trying something new. Besides all that, I absolutely love this songspell, and actually singing on it would be something to remember for the rest of my life.

"Do you have any tricks for when you're nervous performing?" I question.

There's a moment of silence from Snabe, then some faint shuffling. Seconds later, the muscular parasaurolophus appears in the window before me, shirtless.

"Oh my god," I blurt in a fit of laughter.

"Just imagine the audience is naked," he calls out playfully.

I can only see his upper half through the window, but I now realize the dinosaur is completely nude. There's plenty to look at, regardless, his incredible chest and abs just as impressive to gaze upon as the day I first saw them.

I open my mouth in an attempt to come up with some witty reply, but the words refuse to come as my focus remains squarely locked onto Snabe's beautiful physique and the gorgeous, colorful tattoos that line his scaly arms.

"Is it working?" Snabe continues, because you're just as quiet as before.

I smile, shaking my head as I laugh to myself.

"Maybe you should try getting naked, too," Snabe suggests.

I take off my headphones and hang them up on the microphone stand next to me. Slowly, I get to work pulling my shirt up over the top of my head, my heart slamming hard in my chest as I reveal my body to the powerfully attractive parasaurolophus.

I've never been more thankful that I happened to wear my cute underwear.

Snabe watches me move with rapt attention, just as caught up in the moment as I am. There's something utterly intoxicating about this moment, and I'm suddenly reveling in the shift of social dynamics. While I'm normally the one completely swooning over Snabe, I now have him in the palm of my hand.

Realizing this, I hesitate for a moment while unbuttoning my jeans.

I look up and lock eyes with the dinosaur bard. "Like this?" I coo, my voice muffled through the closed studio door, but feeling very sexy all the same.

Snabe nods.

I continue to strip, slipping my jeans down and then gracefully stepping out of them. I'm in nothing but my bra and panties now, rock hard as I continue with the show. I gradually peel those away until I'm completely exposed.

Snabe steps away from the window.

"Hey!" I call out, confused. "Aren't you gonna come in here and have your way with me?"

I suddenly hear the track start up again in my headphones, the song faintly spilling out into the room from their position on my microphone stand. Not knowing what else to do, I hurry back over to the swirling orb and pick them up, placing them over my ears once more.

I've just barely made it in time for the chorus, but when it arrives I'm ready.

I open my mouth and begin to sing, the words spilling out like a soft river of velvet. I feel completely safe in this moment, putting everything I've got into this simple repetitive refrain of my own name. Eventually, the chorus ends, leaving me to stand in silence while the next verse plays out.

I let the music envelope me, swaying my nude hips from side to side with my eyes closed tight. When the next chorus comes I begin again, singing along with the beautiful melody of the songspell. At this point, I'm completely lost in the music, and the next thing I know I'm harmonizing, creating a new but equally beautiful set of pitches to go along with what's already there.

This next chorus goes on three times as long, eventually leading to the end of the spell. When the music finally fades away I return from my trance, feeling strangely satisfied.

The door opens up and Snabe steps inside, closing it softly behind him. He strolls towards me as my eyes drift down to the cock he has equipped.

"That was amazing," Snabe tells me with a wide grin. "We got the take. You even did harmonies! This spell is going to be very potent."

"I did?" I repeat back to him, the whole thing seeming like some kind of strange, surreal dream.

"Yep," the dinosaur says, gently taking my headphones off and hanging them next to me.

I gaze up at him, completely locked into this moment as the man wraps his huge, muscular arms around me and pulls me close. Our lips meet, sending a shockwave of arousal through my body. I'm shaking, the powerful sensations that pulse through me just too much for my small frame to take.

Down below, I can feel Snabe's cock pushing against my hip. I reach down and grip Snabe's thick rod between my slender fingers.

A soft gasp escapes the parasaurolophus's lips as he reels from my gentle touch, craving even more but forced to be patient as I dole out the pleasure to him gradually. I start to pump my hand up and down across Snabe's length, watching intently as his expression reacts to even the subtlest movements. I'm in complete control.

Not for long, though.

Eventually, Snabe begins to play with my most sensitive areas in return, gently stroking me in in a series of perfectly executed movements. It's as though the man knows me better than I know myself, pacing himself with incredible accuracy.

My face flushed red, I'm forced to stop stroking Snabe's rod, much too focused on my own blossoming pleasure. With each passing second I'm becoming even more consumed by warm, aching sensation.

Eventually, Snabe pushes me back, positioning my body on one of the large guitar amps. I sit on the sturdy black cabinet, my legs spread open as the muscular musician kneels down before me. He begins to suck me, immediately getting to work with his mouth as I lean back against the wall behind me.

I reach down and run my hands through Snabe's long black hair, loving every moment of the way that he services my body and soul.

Deep down in the pit of my stomach, a flower has started to bloom, it's pedals unfurling slowly and basking in the pleasurable light that pours down onto them. As Snabe sucks away, these flowers continue to bloom, vines creeping their way down my arms and legs, filling my body with satisfaction and an escalating tension. The pressure grows until I feel as though there's just not enough room left in my body, quaking hard as clench my teeth tight and let out a long, anxious hiss.

"I'm so fucking close," I finally groan, but Snabe already knows this. The dinosaur is right here with me, picking up on every signal that I'm sending his way. He's an attentive lover, singularly focused on giving me pleasure that I so desperately crave.

Snabe keeps up the pace of his pumping lips, and seconds later I'm erupting with orgasmic sensation, my entire body convulsing wildly as it's completely overwhelmed. There's simply too much happening for me to maintain my composure, lost is a tidal wave of climax that turns my mind upside down and inside out. I feel as though I've left my body completely, hovering above myself for a moment when the feelings surging through my body are just too much to take.

Finally, I return to my physical frame, the orgasm passing and leaving me in a state of utter shock. I'm completely satisfied in a way that I never thought possible.

"That was incredible," I gush.

"More?" Snabe questions, pulling back from between my legs and looking up at me with a mischievous grin.

I remember our first time together in the woods, then realize I don't have my wand on me.

"I mean... I can't cast *Sexualis Secondus,*" I trail off, considering his offer. "I don't have my wand."

Snabe scoffs. "You don't need it."

I glance down and notice that I'm already getting hard again on nothing but sheer arousal. No magic needed.

"I want you inside my pussy, though," I tell him.

The next thing I know, Snabe has stood up and pulled me along with him. We kiss briefly, reconnecting for a moment in this midst of this sexual avalanche.

"Thank you," Snabe says, two words that could be referencing a myriad of different things at the point. Regardless, I completely understand want he means, and nod in return.

Suddenly, Snabe is turning me around, leaning me back over the amplifier so that I face away from him. The hulking dinosaur sets up into position behind me, aligning himself carefully before thrusting forward in one slow, confident swoop.

I let out a satisfied groan as Snabe enters me, struggling to come to terms with his incredible size. When I finally do, however, the fullness is gratifying in a way that I can only barely begin to describe.

I feel whole.

Snabe quickly gets to work pumping in and out of me, his parasaurolophus mannerisms much more wild and animalistic than the encounter we had before. He's getting lost in the moment, consumed by desire as he passionately takes me from behind.

Meanwhile, I'm bracing myself against the amp, gazing back over my shoulder at Snabe and loving every second of it. Somehow, despite the speed of his movements, Snabe still manages to hit me in just the right way, aligning his cock so that the pleasure it provides is simply uncontainable. It doesn't take long for me to explode with orgasm yet again, screaming out wildly as every part of my body swells with a second helping of pleasure. This time, however, Snabe reaches climax along with me.

The two of us suddenly push together tightly and hold, writhing with pleasure until finally the sensation passes and leaves us utterly exhausted. I gaze back over my shoulder, locking eyes with the scaly green dinosaur bard and then kissing him deeply on the lips.

CRASH

9

Sometimes the world moves slowly, painstakingly dragging you along with it while every moment stretches on and on for what seems like forever. This typically occurs when you'd rather be anywhere else.

Other times, however, time really does fly.

Ironically, these are the moments that we wish would stick around. The days when everything really does just feel like it's perfectly falling into place.

Ever since me and Snabe got back together, things have felt like this, the wonderful moments cascading by like a river over beautiful rocks, refining their edges and polishing them up, but never quite sticking around as long as you'd like.

Since recording backup vocals on Snabe's spellsong, we've gotten to work bringing his entire studio up to my mountaintop cottage, high above the water's edge and far from any memories that are less than pleasant. I'm not trying to ignore the past, but I'd rather not wallow in it, and I think Snabe is feeling exactly the same way.

Our days have fallen into a routine, but it's a beautiful, glorious one. While the handsome bard records his next album of spells inside, I find myself sitting on the deck while I spellcraft, scribbling away at magical parchment while the inspiration flows through me. The weather's turned for the better, and it's been remarkably warm during what could've been a chilly season.

Eventually, Snabe will take a break and come out to sit with me, venting about the incantations that he's trying to smooth out or the chord changes that aren't quite right yet, while I explain to him my own issues with components and rituals.

It might sound like we're being nothing but critical, but that couldn't be further from the truth. Snabe is the sounding board that I've always wanted, brutally honest and open, but with a kindness in his heart that makes things easier to hear. We tell each other exactly what we think, but have found ourselves in the fortunate situation of absolutely loving one another's projects. When Snabe plays me a new spellsong that he's working on, I know he wants the truth.

Obviously, I'm willing to give it to him, but his bardic chants all happen to be really damn good.

Clearly, were not the only ones who think that about each other's art. Over the last few weeks, Morgan Phoenix Spellcrafting and their new head wizard have been losing their minds over my new ritual, which is now edging dangerously close to a finished scroll.

Meanwhile, Snabe's bardic record label has been pushing for more tracks, absolutely thrilled with the response to *Harriet Metamalium*. The leaked demo went viral almost instantly, and when the finished spellsong was sent out days later as a fully produced single, Seven Inch Nails was definitely back on the map.

Now the suits are calling day and night, hoping to release a new full-length record as soon as possible, and they've fortunately caught Snabe during a very productive phase. I'm not entirely sure when he'll be ready, but from the sound of it, the guys back in Bristol won't have to wait long.

Of course, it's not just the professional side of things that's going well around here. Snabe and me have been going at it like jackrabbits, having more sex than I would've ever thought a dinosaur was capable of providing.

Typically, when I'm at a good place in my life I'm damn near insatiable, but Snabe is giving me a run for my money.

We still make time to get out of the house, heading down to Captain Orion's Cove for dinner whenever we want a brief moment away from the cabin. It's nice to see Gobby, who still apologizes profusely for not warning me about Snabe's surprise romantic concert, but I wave her away. Everything worked out just fine.

This is the way our island lives go for quite some time, a man and a woman proving that you're not required to be endlessly tortured to make great spells. Of course, it remains to be seen whether or not people out there in the real world decide to pick up what we're putting down, but at least we're giving it our best shot.

Like all things, however, these carefree days must eventually come to an end.

This is that moment, I realize, the moment when everything turns.

I'm standing in the doorway of our cottage in the early afternoon, hoping to step outside with a cold cup of chocolate milk but halting in my tracks when something blocks my path.

My eyes remain glued on the ground before me, trying to wrap my mind around what could've possibly done this.

There on the deck are the bloody remains of what appears to be a small, woodland animal, still fresh and sticky from the brief glance I get before looking away.

"Snabe!" I cry out. "Come look at this!"

Moments later, the protective dinosaur comes bounding out from the other room. He wraps his arm around me, but instantly notices my chilly response to his touch. Snabe glances down and stops in his tracks exactly like I did.

"Well, that's not something you see every day," the man observes.

"What is it?" I question, utterly disgusted.

Snabe shakes his head. "Some kind of three-headed animal. Maybe a rabbit or a fox, they're all over the island."

"Do you think a wolf could've done this?" I continue.

"No wolves on the island," Snabe informs me. "No large predators at all, actually. That's why there's so many damn foxes. There's hungry hawks around here, but this is a little too big for them, especially with the three heads."

I narrow my eyes. "What are you saying? That a person did this?"

"I mean... what else?" Snabe counters.

I suddenly turn my attention to the woods around us, my eyes scanning across the tree line for a glimpse of anyone who might be watching from afar.

"Should we call the police?" I wonder aloud.

Snabe considers this for a moment. "I don't think so. I don't know what they'd do for us. Honestly, it's probably nothing. An animal could've just curled up and died here looking for some shelter."

A scoff. "That's not what an animal looks like when it just curls up and dies."

Snabe lets out a long sigh. "Fair enough. You want me to get the sheriff out here to take a look?"

I appreciate that Snabe is willing to humor me like this, but he actually has a point. This is a long way from town for the island's only law enforcement to come pay us a quick visit, and he won't have much to go on.

"It's fine," I finally offer.

"You sure?" the parasaurolophus continues, deeply concerned about doing the right thing for me.

"I'm sure," I tell him, forcing a smile.

Snabe nods. "You know, an animal could've be hit by a car down on the main road, then made its way up here before kicking the bucket."

"Or a motorcycle," I offer.

The two of us stand in silence for a moment.

"You get started with your writing," Snabe offers. "I'll sing this off and you'll never have to think about it again."

I wrap my arms around the beautiful, tattoo covered dinosaur and kiss him deeply, thankful to have found such a caring guy by my side. He's still a little rough around the edges, of course, but when it comes to dealing with me, Snabe is nothing but a gentleman these days.

I stay like this in my muscular lover's embrace, while he gets to work. The parasaurolophus clears his throat and then begins to sing a cleaning incantation. I watch as swirling splashes of water begin to manifest in the air before us then rush across the ground, pulling the carnage off into the woods and then scrubbing down the place where the animal carcass had been left.

By the time Snabe finishes with his simple bardic chant there's nothing left.

"Thanks," I offer with a smile, then head back out to the deck.

I sit down in my usual chair, overlooking the glorious cascade of evergreens and the cliffs below. This has become a place of peace and endless inspiration, but now I find myself deeply disturbed. No matter how many times I tell myself that the carnage at the front door was nothing to be worried about, I still can't push it completely out of my mind.

That mess could've been cause by a number of things, but there's only one motor vehicle I can think of who would actually follow through with it.

Snabe raps gently on the wooden doorframe behind me. "All done," he tells me. "I'm headed back into the studio."

"Already?" I question, turning around in my chair.

Snabe nods.

I realize suddenly that I've been lost in thought for at least fifteen minutes, completely zoned out as I allowed my mind to wander.

"Are you okay?" the dinosaur asks, picking up on the subtle cues of my body language.

I take a deep breath, trying to align my thoughts calmly and not erupt like a blathering lunatic.

"You think it's Dellatrix, don't you," Snabe eventually offers.

I nod. "You can't tell me that didn't cross your mind."

The muscular parasaurolophus sticks out his bottom lip, thinking quietly to himself. "I saw her leave the island. I drove her to the airport myself."

I narrow my eyes. "There's an airport here?"

"It's small," Snabe informs me. "Very small."

"You don't think she could've turned around and hopped a plane right back?" I counter. "Maybe she got ahold of a teleportation scroll."

"Sure. She could have," Snabe concedes. "But those are rare and expensive. I ran out last year and I still haven't been able to get ahold of any more. Regardless, I just don't really think she's *that* crazy. I mean, don't get me wrong, she's absolutely mad, but I don't know if she's the type to kill a three headed fox and leave it on someone's front porch."

"I don't know either," I admit.

"Well, we'll keep an eye out," the parasaurolophus finally concludes. "That's all we can do. Don't let her keep ruining your day after she's long gone."

The loving dinosaur strolls over and kisses me on my forehead. He stays here for a moment, resting his comforting reptilian hands on my shoulders, and then eventually heads back inside, shutting the door to his makeshift studio behind him.

I take a deep breath and let my gaze return to the parchment before me, struggling to begin and desperately hoping that once my pen gets going my subconscious brain will do the rest. I've come too far to let this spell slow down now, just a small bit of tweaking left before crossing the finish line.

I force myself to dive in.

I pick up my wand and wave it in the air. "Miricalum onoso patrolin!" I announce, focusing on the page after page of instructions and incantations I've been pouring over for ages now.

I sizzle of magical energy announces itself at the tip of my wand, causing a wide smile to erupt across my face. Moments later, however, it disappears.

"Did it work?" I question aloud, glancing at my wand, then the parchment, then my wand yet again.

It doesn't look like it. For a spell this powerful, there's gotta be a bigger show than that. I take a deep breath, then start troubleshooting.

Somehow, I actually manage to get a little work done today, although it's much more difficult than I'm used to. As the sun creeps slowly across the sky above, I find my mind wandering, drifting back to the mysterious gift that was left for us this morning. I try my best not to think about it, realizing that if this is the work of some disgruntled motorcycle, my distraction and fear is exactly what they want.

Meanwhile, Snabe continues writing and recording from deep within the cottage, the sound of his spellsongs just barely audible through the thick door we've installed. The fact that he cares enough to keep the volume down these days fills me with so many pleasant feelings, they eventually push out the bad vibes completely.

By the time dinner rolls around, Dellatrix is once again a distant memory.

"You hungry?" Snabe questions, sneaking up behind me.

I don't hesitate for a second, closing down my laptop rolling up my parchment before standing abruptly. "Hell yes," I reply.

I carry my spellcrafting tools back inside and pack them away safely, then grab a jacket, taking great care to make sure that every door and window is closed and locked. I even cast a little protection hex on my own wand, just in case.

Soon enough, Snabe and me are climbing into his car and taking off down the hill, the same drive we've made a hundred times before. It's become routine now, something that neither of us think twice about as we navigate the curves that wind up and down our tree-filled cliffside route.

The angle is steep and the turns are sharp, but there's never much of a problem if you take things slow.

Today, Snabe's not taking things slow.

"Come on," I blurt out suddenly, glancing over at the dinosaur with a look of frustration.

I'd rather he never drove like this, and when he's on his own there's nothing I can do. If I'm a passenger in the car, however, I have no problem telling Snabe to slow the hell down.

Everything changes when I see Snabe's expression. The parasaurolophus is just as concerned as I am, his visible mixture of fear and confusion drastically elevating with every passing second.

"Slow down!" I yell, struggling to understand why Snabe would be acting this way.

The dinosaur shakes his head frantically, now slamming his foot down over and over again on the brakes. Nothing happens.

"I can't stop!" Snabe cries out.

I left my main wand at home, but fortunately I keep a spare in the glove compartment. Frantically, I tear it open and begin searching frantically through the registration and insurance papers within, desperate for this powerful tool. I know more than a few spells that can slow us down, but I'll need to find a wand before I can cast them.

We're coming up on the first switchback dangerously fast now, and without much time to consider his options, Snabe yanks the wheel as hard as he possibly can. We round the bend with a loud screech, just a few feet shy of careening over the edge.

The second the dinosaur does this I notice my spare wand fly out of the glove compartment and through the window of the car.

I can feel the weight of the car tipping slightly, threatening to flip over completely but somehow managing to stay upright as we make the turn. For once, I'm actually thankful to be in Snabe's low-sitting sports car and not some top-heavy ride, otherwise we might've ended up tumbling over the cliff.

Unfortunately, there are several more turns coming up, and we've done nothing but gain speed. The trees are flying past us on either side now, the weight of our vehicle taking over and propelling us onward at an ever-escalating pace.

Suddenly, Snabe's survival instincts kick in. Instead of going into even more of a full-on panic, the man becomes eerily calm. He begins to chant to myself softly, reciting an old and rarely used incantation to the best of his abilities. The car begins to slow while a loud grinding sound fills our ears.

Wisps of magical energy begin to erupt from the tires in plumes of sparkling blue light.

Unfortunately, it's just not enough to stop us completely after all the momentum we've built up on this steep incline. Somehow we still manage to make the next turn, however, whipping around the bend.

We now find ourselves at the top of a long straightaway, ending in a final turn that also happens to be the sharpest of the bunch. The road here is so steep that even the songspell is having trouble slowing us down.

I can tell this isn't a bardic incantation Snabe uses very often. He's messing up the words, and the magic is only doing half its job.

"Hold on tight," Snabe sudden tells me, breaking away from his chant and glancing over to make sure my seatbelt is firmly secured.

Realizing that we'll only be speeding up from here, Snabe cocks the wheel slightly and heads off into the dirt, dust and debris spraying everywhere. He's aiming for the smallest tree he can find, something with a little give, but when we hit the tall, deeply rooted trunk, we might as well be slamming into a brick wall.

There's a deafening bang as an airbag goes off next to me, filling the left side of Snabe's Jag with a puffy white cloud. Meanwhile, my side of the car fills with shattering glass, a renegade branch punching a massive hole through the windshield and nearly impaling my face. My entire body snaps forward as the seatbelts lock tight, securing me in place but damn near yanking my shoulder out from its socket. I'm completely overwhelmed with searing pain.

Then, in less than the space of a single second, it's all over.

Dust begins to settle around me as I cough, each heave of my chest filling my body with excruciating pain. I'm bewildered and disoriented, struggling to understand my orientation in the world as a high-pitched ring annihilates my ears.

I'm vaguely aware of the airbag moving around next to me, then moments later my passenger door opens.

Snabe is hovering over my wounded body, his mouth moving but the words not making any sense. He's repeating the same question over and over again, but I don't understand what it is so I just stare back at him in a state of shock.

Moments later, Snabe is reaching in and unbuckling my seatbelt. The dinosaur wraps his huge, muscular arms around me and carefully lifts me up from my seat, safety glass spilling away from my lap. Instinctually, I cling to Snabe's broad chest, holding on tight as he begins to carry me, step by step, back up the hill.

"What's happening?" I groan.

Snabe shakes his head. "I don't know. The brakes stopped working."

"Someone cut them," I continue.

"Yeah," Snabe affirms with a nod. "They turned off the passenger side airbag, too."

I close my eyes and snuggle deep into Snabe's chest, enjoying his scaly comfort at a time when I need it the most. Despite everything that just happened, I still somehow feel safe in his parasaurolophus arms.

There's no question now that someone is out to get me, and Dellatrix is the number one suspect, but I honestly believe that Snabe will protect me from harm. Hell, I've got no problem protecting myself.

In the meantime, I need to rest.

"Looks like we're having dinner at home tonight," Snabe offers.

"Yay," I reply meekly, the single word drenched in sarcasm.

Snabe forces a smile; his pace not faltering for a second as he continues to carry me up the road in his arms.

From my place in the bedroom and can hear Snabe and the unicorn sheriff talking quietly, their voices full of concern as they struggle to determine where to go from here. Snabe seems frustrated, and it's understandable why. If I wasn't aching from head to toe while buried under an ocean of warm blankets, I'd be frustrated too, but right now I'm still focused on trying to exist comfortably in my own body.

The problem, it seems, is that there's not much we can actually do about our situation. As far as anyone is aware, Dellatrix is not on the island, and what Snabe knows of her vehicle registration is so vague and undefined that it's impossible to get a restraining order. She's gone under several last names, apparently, all of them fake. The motorcycle is like a ghost.

Besides, there's still no direct evidence linking her to any of this. Of course, it fits her personality to a tee, but that's just not enough in the eyes of the law.

After investigating the wreckage, it's determined that the brake line was, in fact, cut. The passenger side airbag was also intentionally deactivated.

All of this has culminated in Snabe making a call to his old woolly mammoth bodyguard from back in the day when Seven Inch Nails were at their peak, a prehistoric friend who Snabe claims to trust with his life. They've known each other since magic school.

Apparently, he'll be here within the next few days.

The doctor came by earlier, providing me with some incredibly potent healing potions and stern instructions to rest for the next two weeks. While no bones were broken, my rib cage is horribly bruised and my head is concussed. If this was the big city there would be expert healing wizards readily available, but out here on the island I'll have to make due with a few potions and some good rest.

Sitting at my bedside, the doctor observes this is the second head injury I've been around for, although the first one happened to a motorcycle.

"Dellatrix did that to herself," I informed the doctor. "I found the boat paddle."

He seemed unconvinced. "A welt like that? I doubt it."

I furrowed my brow. "Why?"

"People don't realize how difficult it is to hit yourself that hard," the doctor explained. "Your brain will always try to pull back at the last second. Unless you're drunk on chocolate milk, of course."

"Well, there you go," I reply.

Out in the living room, Sheriff Thomson finally leaves, the unicorn instructing Snabe to give him a call if he notices anything suspicious and also mentions hoping nobody drinks his blood for a second time, which is weird. Down on the road below, a crew has almost finished clearing away Snabe's smashed up car, the front half crunched in on itself like an aluminum can.

Snabe enters the bedroom quietly, walking over and kneeling down at the edge of the bed. He takes my hands in his claws and then kisses them softly, a gesture that feels both beautiful and strange coming from such a large, muscular dinosaur.

"I'm so sorry," Snabe finally says.

"It's not your fault," I assure him.

"It is," he continues. "I should've never let a sentient motorcycle like that into my life."

I crack a smile. "Maybe it is a *little bit* your fault."

Snabe leans in and gives me a quick kiss. "Well, at least you still have a good sense of humor about things."

"I kinda have to," I retort.

Snabe nods, then takes in a deep breath, his mind shifting elsewhere. "Sheriff Thomson says they're investigating. Whatever that means."

"They?" I reply. "You mean there's more than one person fighting crime on this island?"

"Sounds like it," Snabe continues. "He says we shouldn't tell anyone about what happened. Apparently, that makes it even harder to pin down any suspects. The press will go absolutely nuts with this."

"Wow, yeah," I reply, truly realizing for the first time how much people care about the minutia of Snabe's life. As a wizard I've got a fan base of my own, too, albeit quite a bit smaller, but the combination of me and my new rockstar bard boyfriend in a fight for our lives would quickly ignite the wizarding press.

Suddenly, another thought crosses my mind. "Are you my boyfriend?" I question, realizing that it's an important discussion we've never quite gotten around to.

Snabe smiles. "Do you want me to be?"

I nod.

"Of course I'm your boyfriend," the parasaurolophus replies, giving my hand a brief squeeze.

I close my eyes, basking in this moment a bit. It's funny that we've grow so close without actually saying the words *boyfriend* or *girlfriend*. I guess all it takes is a near death experience.

"I won't tell anyone about the crash," I finally say, "but it's gonna be so hard with all these people coming and going."

Snabe laughs and rolls his eyes at my sarcastic exaggeration. "I'm gonna start making dinner, you need anything?"

I smile wide, impressed. "*You're* gonna start making dinner?" I question. "The bad bard of Britain? Snabe Rezmor himself? Making me dinner?"

"I didn't say it was going to be good," Snabe jokes.

"Well, I'm excited to find out," I tell him, then suddenly my mood shifts to one of deep seriousness. "Just make sure the door and windows are locked."

"I will," Snabe assures me, standing up.

"When's your mammoth bodyguard gonna get here?" I ask.

"As soon as he can, and he's your bodyguard now, too," Snabe reminds me.

AN OLD FRIEND

10

It's pitch black when I wake, but I know exactly where I am. I can feel it.

I'm in the old cabin by the water, once warm and cozy but now filled with a sense of creeping dread. I sit up in bed, my heart slamming hard within my chest as I realize that someone is in the house.

I haven't heard them yet, nor seen them, but I know in the bottom of my heart that they're out in the living room, waiting for me to confront them.

I stand, walking through the darkness of the bedroom towards the door, then stop when a spotlight appears before me, shining brilliant and illuminating an oar that leans propped up against the wall. I reach out and take the wooden paddle in my hand, recognizing it immediately. Dellatrix's blood is still on it, only now the blood is fresh, glistening under the hot white light that shines down from above.

Somehow, I know that my wand is missing.

The spotlight shuts off with a loud clang and I continue on my way, brandishing the oar over my shoulder like a weapon as I slowly pull open the bedroom door with my other hand. I peer out into the living room, which has been flooded with luminous blue stage lighting.

Dellatrix is idling there before me, but the motorcycle is facing away, turned to gaze longingly out the windows and down towards the beach.

In the sky above this beautiful night landscape hangs an oversized yellow moon, but it's flat and painted, the craters too large to be real. It sways ever so slightly in the air, as if dangling from a long strand of fishing wire.

"What the hell are you doing in here," I demand to know, addressing this darkened figure directly.

Dellatrix says nothing, doesn't even move as she realizes she's been caught red handed. Instead, the motorbike just continues to stare out into the darkness of the quiet night before her.

"Get out of my house," I command.

Still, Dellatrix does nothing.

My heart is pounding harder than ever now, completely taken aback by the bizarreness of this situation. The way that Dellatrix is acting is utterly surreal, as if in a trace.

Slowly, I begin to creep forward, lowing my oar and reaching out with a trembling hand. Closer and closer I drift, until eventually I'm standing right behind the silent figure.

I place my hand on Dellatrix's shoulder.

Suddenly, the motorbike spins around, revealing an absolutely horrific visage. It's Dellatrix alright, but her skin is paper white with hints of frozen blue. She's wet and waterlogged, her eyes completely black while her mouth hangs agape and a small, deep sea crab crawls forth.

I scream, falling back a bit and instinctually swinging my oar at Dellatrix's face as hard as I can.

Suddenly, I'm back in my own bedroom, not the one at the original cabin but up on the hill with Snabe. I sit upright once more and gasp loudly, the movement sending a shockwave of pain across my bruised chest.

Confused and disoriented, I glance over and see Snabe lying silently in the bed next to me, his bare green shoulders exposed to reveal a colorful and intricate avalanche of tattoos.

Based on the light that's beginning to stream through our windows, it's dawn, and while I should definitely be getting as much rest as I possibly can, I also know that I won't be able to get back to sleep no matter how long I lay here.

Careful not to wake Snabe, I pull off the covers and climb out of bed, creeping to the kitchen and pulling out a carton of chocolate milk.

I pour myself a tall glass and then take a sip.

My *boyfriend*, I remind myself.

I smile, excited by the way that it feels to think that, to officially recognize the connection we have with a real title.

The chocolate milk is nice and warm within my throat. It's been two days since the accident, and I still feel as though my respiratory system is covered in dust and dirt from the inside out.

"You make enough for me?" Snabe asks from the doorway.

The dinosaur is still shirtless, his glorious chest and abs rippling as he moves towards me. The parasaurolophus is so toned that looking at him is like admiring an anatomy book, every muscular connection making perfect sense within his body. I can see the way that his stomach flexes when he breathes, the swaying of his lower abdominals when he strolls forward.

"See something you like?" Snabe jokes.

"You know it," I tell him, wrapping my arms around his scaly body and tilting my head up to kiss him passionately on the mouth.

"Tastes good," Snabe says with a smile.

"Extra sweet," I offer. "Right up your alley."

Snabe walks over and inspects the milk carton, smirking a little. "Well, that's a lot of added sugar."

"You said it tasted good!" I retort.

"I said *you* taste good," Snabe replies.

I laugh. "Fair enough."

The forest around us continues to grow lighter and lighter with every passing second, the sound of chirping birds now drifting out across my ears.

For almost dying a few days ago, I'm feeling remarkably at ease now.

"You're up early," Snabe observes.

"I had a nightmare," I inform the dinosaur.

"Oh yeah?" Snabe replies. "Well, it couldn't be any more frightening than a stalker cutting your brakes, now could it?"

"Actually, yeah," I reply. "Dellatrix was there, but she looked like she'd been floating under a frozen lake for weeks."

"That *is* creepy," Snabe affirms. "What did she do?"

"Nothing really," I continue, "but I hit her in the face with an oar."

"That's my girl," Snabe says with a laugh, putting his arm around me and pulling me close. Suddenly his expression gets serious. "Are you gonna be okay here while I'm at the concert?"

"If your bodyguard ever shows up," I reply.

The second that I say this, two headlights come slicing up through the soft light of the morning. A black sedan soon pulls up to the side of the cabin.

"There you go," Snabe continues with a laugh, strolling past me and heading out into the cool morning air.

A huge woolly mammoth climbs out of the car and greets Snabe with a powerful hug. His hair is scraggly and white, and he's wearing a tall, wizardly hat that demands respect.

They exchange a few words before Snabe returns through the front door of the cabin, bringing our guest along with him.

"Harriet, this is Bumbleborn," Snabe informs me. "We went to magic school together back in the day."

Bumbleborn reaches out an enormous furry hand and I give him a firm shake. I like this guy already. While plenty of prehistoric creatures Bumbleborn's size can be imposing and downright scary, Bumbleborn carries himself like a gentle giant. The expressions on his face are deeply concerned, almost frightened, betraying his enormous and powerful body. I have no question, however, that he's got what it takes to defend me, especially when I notice the wand-sized bulge tucked safely within the side of his leather jacket.

"I'm gay," Bumbleborn says.

"Uh... what?" I stammer, a little confused. "That's cool."

"I just wanted to say that clearly in this story instead of claiming years later it was there in the subtext the whole time," the woolly mammoth continues.

"That's awesome," I reply with a smile, only half following this conversation that's clearly steeped in metamagic.

"So, you're the girl that finally made him settle down, huh?" Bumbleborn asks me, his voice shockingly deep.

"I guess so," I confirm with a nod.

"He needed it," Bumbleborn confirms, then glances over at Snabe. "I hope that doesn't mean you can't crack open a cold chocolate milk with me for old time's sake."

"I just tasted some on my girlfriend's lips," Snabe finally says, "I think that's enough chocolate milk for me."

"Fair enough," Bumbleborn replies. "I'll keep my milk stash in the trunk."

"Oh, you don't have to do that," I interject. "There's plenty of room in the fridge."

Bumbleborn shakes his head. "I know better than to tempt him when he's like this," the bodyguard explains. "When Snabe swings back, he swings back hard."

I can't help letting this comment slice deep into my heart, sending an icy chill of fear surging out through my veins. I hadn't considered how many *other* times Snabe might've tried to change his ways, that all of the progress we'd made together wasn't yet beyond a bad boy relapse.

For the last few weeks, I'd assumed we were well past the finish line, celebrating together after a hard won victory over his asshole tendencies. Now, I realize that we're still in the race.

Bumbleborn excuses himself, heading back out to the car to gather his bags.

"What did he mean by that?" I question, turning to the dinosaur.

"By what?" the bard replies, genuinely confused.

"About you swinging back hard," I question. "I thought we were done with all that bad boy romance trope stuff. It's toxic, remember?"

A wave of deep emotional weight suddenly crosses my boyfriend's face as he turns to me, staring deep into my eyes. "I'm never entirely done with this stuff. It's a part of me, and the second that I tell myself I'm done trying is the second it all comes back. That's just how romance novels work. Do you understand?"

I shake my head. "Maybe this doesn't have to be a romance novel. Maybe it can be a fantasy?"

"It's Chuck Tingle," Snabe offers. "Even though there's gonna be plenty of meta commentary letting you know his opinions on this toxic trope, It's still probably gonna be a little of both. I'm sorry," he apologizes with great sincerity.

I shake my head. "It's fine, I just didn't know."

I realize now the incredible feat that Snabe has been performing for me.

I've been well aware of the effort this dinosaur has put in, and without it he wouldn't have won me back. What I didn't really consider, however, is how well Snabe has kept his internal bad boy struggles to himself, not wanting to burden me with the daily cravings that he will forever keep at bay. His attitude is in check, and his choices are positive, but that doesn't mean he's not fighting with every ounce of his soul to keep it that way.

This weekend, Snabe is heading to Dublin for a concert and some bardic meetings, while I'm stuck back here at the cabin with a strict order from my doctor to rest and recuperate. With all the drama and danger surrounding Dellatrix's return, we've been worried about my safety in the forest. Now, however, I'm starting to worry about Snabe's safety in the big city.

Bumbleborn comes back inside and walks his bag over to the couch. "This seems like a good place for me," he announces. "I've got a view of the front door and I'm just a few feet from the bedroom."

"Perfect," Snabe confirms with a nod.

Bumbleborn thinks to himself for a moment, then smiles wide and stretches out his long trunk happily. "It's good to be back," he finally says. "When was the last tour, six years ago? Damn."

"Just about," Snabe replies.

"The new songspell is really good," Bumbleborn continues. "I mean, you know I don't usually go for that soft shit, but it's good. It's all over the radio now, man."

Snabe laughs. "Yeah, it kinda came outta nowhere."

"And now you're back on top!" Bumbleborn cries. "Wizards love it! Warlocks love it! Bards love it! Just like the good old days!"

"Not quite," my boyfriend assures him.

"Fair enough," Bumbleborn replies with a wink and a nod, then turns his attention to me. "You inspired a hell of a magic spell. You saved this dinosaur's career."

I laugh. "I guess I never really thought of it that way."

"It's true," Snabe confirms, the parasaurolophus putting his arm around me and kissing me gently on the side of the head.

Bumbleborn takes a deep breath, looking around the room and getting the lay of the land. "I'm gonna take a walk around the property," he finally announces. "I've got a few magic eyes I'd like to set up, too."

The mammoth pulls a small, floating eyeball out of his pocket, a security based magic item that most notable wizardly locations make use of.

Snabe gives him an affirmative nod. "Sounds good."

"What time are you headed to the airport?" Bumbleborn questions.

Snabe pulls out his phone to check the time. "Soon," he replies. "Early flight."

"Well, I'll be back in time to say goodbye," Bumbleborn continues, standing up again and strolling past us. He pushes out the front door and starts to make his way around the house, scouting things out in a militaristic way that I can only barely begin to understand.

"See, you'll be fine here," Snabe assures me.

"I'm not worried about myself," I inform him.

Snabe pulls back a bit, checking my expression. "What are you worried about?"

"I know how hard it is for you to settle down like this," I explain. "I know the effort you're putting in right now."

"Thank you," he replies with a smile, "but I'll be fine."

"Honestly, I just wish I could see you play," I admit. "I haven't seen a Seven Inch Nails performance in years."

"We haven't *performed* in years," Snabe replies with a laugh. "The band's been rehearsing non-stop, though. I think we're gonna kill it."

I let out a long sigh, my mind immediately beginning to extrapolate this comment, stretching it out into a myriad of potential futures for us as a couple.

"And then what?" I ask him.

"What do you mean?" Snabe replies. "Then I'll come back here and finish the new record of songspells! You'll be right here with me!"

"No, I mean after that," I continue. "One show leads to more shows, which leads to tours and temptation. Are you ready for that?"

Snabe gives my words the weight they deserve and then smiles. "Of course I'm ready for that. I'll have you by my side."

I'm confused. "What?"

"You don't think you can write a spell from the road?" Snabe continues. "All you need is that laptop and some parchment."

"I hadn't really thought about it," I stammer, steadily growing more and more excited.

Lately, my thoughts have been deeply wrapped up in the present, which is a fantastic way to spellcraft, but as the future begins to make its way into my current reality, I find myself pushing back against it. I like what Snabe and me have, and the prospect of that changing is something I'd rather not dwell on. We've overcome too much to get here, meeting in the middle of our personalities and lifestyles to become a productive, happy couple.

I've tried not to think about it, but I know deep down that the better Snabe's spellsong does, the longer he'll be on tour, the more he'll be surrounded by the temptation of that bad boy lifestyle.

I never considered that I'd be invited along.

"I need you there to keep me on track," the dinosaur states, rather bluntly. "I need your help."

"Of course I'll come along," I blurt, swelling with joy.

Snabe nods. "Good."

I take a deep breath, and then realize how much time has passed since we've been standing here. "You need to start packing for your flight," I remind him.

TONIGHT'S THE NIGHT

11

The first day after Snabe leaves is a productive one, consisting mostly of me lying in bed with parchment on my lap as words fly by in beautiful cascades of magical black ink. I'm on fire, synthesizing the drama of my life into a beautiful piece of magic.

I was afraid to be left alone with a stalker on the prowl, but Bumbleborn is a saint and the mammoth makes me feel nothing but safe and protected.

Even my health is improving. While it had been quite painful to move about the cabin just yesterday, I've suddenly found myself incredibly mobile after imbibing the magic potions. The aches have mostly disappeared, along with the swelling and bruises, fading away as my body continues to fight the good fight on my behalf.

By the next day, I'm calling Snabe and telling him I'd like to come to the big show.

"You need to rest," he reminds me, my boyfriend's thick British accent slightly difficult to understand through the static filled cellphone that's pressed against my head. "There's gonna be a hundred of other shows."

"But this is the comeback!" I remind him, leaning forward against the wooden railing of our deck and gazing down into the lush green forest below. "And it's *my* spellsong!"

"You'll be hearing that song for the rest of your life," Snabe informs me. "It's a blessing and a curse. Trust me."

"So you don't want me to come?" I continue.

Snabe lets out a long sigh. "I'd love for you to come, actually, but I'm trying to be responsible here."

"I don't get it," I counter.

"Every day we have a series of choices, some of them good, some bad, and some of them right down the middle. Sometimes it's hard to tell which one is which, but most of the time we know. Do you follow me?" he questions.

"I'm not sure," I admit.

"When I first met you, I was making all the wrong choices, and deep down I knew it," Snabe continues. "My life was falling apart but I didn't care. I'm a bad boy in a romance novel, that's just how I'm written. Every time I'd see those crossroads coming, I'd make the wrong turn. After you left, I told myself I wasn't going to do that anymore. I'm not always gonna know which path is the right one, but I'm gonna try my hardest to make my best guess; the *responsible* guess."

"I appreciate that," I tell him, once again floored but how much effort this man has put into his future; into *our* future.

"I'd love for you to be at the show," Snabe continues, "and the old me would've said 'fuck the doctor's advice, get here as fast as you can,' but that's not the responsible path."

"I can't believe that you're the one telling *me* to be responsible," I laugh. "The whole world is upside down."

Snabe chuckles. "If you really want to come, you should come. I would love to have you here."

I take a deep breath, then let it out, struggling to be inspired by Snabe's maturity. "No, you're right. There's plenty of other shows, and I need to rest."

Through the earpiece of my phone I can hear someone calling out to Snabe.

"Aw fuck," my boyfriend groans. "An interview with Wizards Of The World about to start. They just got here and I can already tell they're gonna be pricks."

"Good choices," I remind him.

"Right, right," Snabe replies, straightening himself out a bit. "How's Bumbleborn, by the way?"

I glance over at the mammoth bodyguard who sits quietly at the edge of the deck, eyes wide open as he diligently scans the tree line.

"Oh, he's amazing," I reply.

"Good," Snabe starts, then suddenly shifts gears. "Okay, gotta run."

The line goes dead.

I put my phone back into my coat pocket and take a minute to draw in the fresh, cool air through my nostrils. It's hard to be responsible, I realize. Even for me.

Not wanting to dive right back into my writing just yet, I glance over at Bumbleborn.

"Wanna go for a walk?" I ask the massive prehistoric wizard.

Bumbleborn nods. "You sure you can do that?'

"I wouldn't say I'm *sure*, but I'd like to see where I'm at," I reply.

Bumbleborn stands up and watches me closely as I make my way across the deck, down onto the front yard and towards the road. My pace is good, actually, no longer any trace of a limp at all. My lungs still feel heavy, but not enough to slow me down.

Bumbleborn falls into step next to me. "You're doing great."

"So far, so good," I reply with confidence.

The two of us make our way down the hill, slowly at first and then gaining speed as I find the confidence behind my step. I quickly realize that most of what's been holding me back is the full day I've spent off my feet, my muscles a little sore and locked up from their lack of use.

"You've done a good thing getting that dinosaur to settle down," Bumbleborn informs me. "I didn't think it was possible, to be honest."

"Oh yeah?" I question. "I'm glad to hear that. I was worried his old friend Bumbleborn would see things differently."

"Nobody likes an asshole," Bumbleborn reminds me. "Snabe has a really good thing buried deep underneath all that bullshit, but I'd rather the bullshit just wasn't there to begin with. Of course, you already know that."

"I do," I offer with a nod.

"I just hope it sticks," Bumbleborn says, almost as an afterthought. I can tell that he regrets the words immediately after they leave his mouth. Bumbleborn's a good friend, and he doesn't want to talk bad about his buddy, especially not to me.

"Why wouldn't it stick?" I question.

The woolly mammoth shakes his head. "I'm just running my mouth now. Snabe's a good dude."

"Why wouldn't it stick?" I ask again, demanding to know.

Still, Bumbleborn refuses to go there. "Just, keep an eye on him," the bodyguard tells me.

"Looks like we've got a similar job," I finally reply with a smile. "Keeping a close eye on a recovering asshole."

Strolling down the hill like this is strangely cathartic. I'm retracing my path towards the big crash, only now I'm in complete control of the situation. The light streaming down through the thick evergreens above is much more glorious when you have a chance to actually take it all in.

Bumbleborn and me arrive at the first switchback, and then the next. Finally, we reach the straightaway where Snabe swerved off the road. All of the metal has been hauled away, but piles of broken glass remain scattered along the hillside and sprinkled over the pavement from when the car was removed. The tree that we hit is still standing, but bent slightly backwards as through it's in the midst of some gleeful cackle. All of the bark has been torn from its trunk, leaving a massive tan slash of exposed flesh underneath.

"Still standing," I observe. "Just like me."

Bumbleborn nods. "You wanna keep walking?" he asks.

"Just a bit farther," I reply, turning to continue down the road.

It's only now that I see it, massive black words splattered out across the ground before us. At first it's hard to tell what the liquid is, but the smell soon gives it away as motor oil. *Motorcycle* oil. I stop dead in my tracks, staring at the words in utter shock.

Tonight's the night, it reads. *P. S. Nice magic eyes.*

"Oh my god," I stammer, immediately on high alert. I begin to glance around in the woods, terrified someone out there might be watching us.

Bumbleborn pulls his wand from his belt with a giant furry hand, not quite ready to raise it just yet, but holding it steady as his eyes remain peeled.

"She's been watching us," I say. "She knows about the eyes."

Bumbleborn just nods, turning and slowly making his way back up the hill.

"Where are you going?" I demand to know.

"To get the car, and you're coming with me," Bumbleborn explains. "We're not staying in the cabin tonight."

A thousand different thoughts are rushing through my head, shifting my focus this way and that. I'm completely overwhelmed, and the only thing that I truly want right now is the safety of Snabe's strong arms.

I pull out my phone and dial Snabe's number. He answers immediately.

"Hey!" the parasaurolophus cries out, excited to hear from me.

"I'm coming to see you tonight," I inform him.

"You need to rest! It's fine!" Snabe counters. "We already talked about this."

"Dellatrix was here, she painted something on the road," I stammer, the primal fear finally seeping out into my voice.

"What?" Snabe blurts, completely thrown. "Is Bumbleborn with you?"

The bodyguard can hear this through the line. "Yeah I'm here," he calls out.

"He's here, but it's still not safe," I continue. "She knows about the eyeballs. She knows about everything."

"Okay, okay," Snabe replies, his reptilian brain kicking into emergency mode. "We need to get you off the island fast."

"I just want to be next to you," I tell him.

"There's no flights to Dublin left," the worried mammoth continues, thinking out loud, then suddenly shifts gears. "I know what to do!"

"What is it?" I question.

"Braco is taking the boat to the show!" Snabe continues. "You and Bumbleborn can ride with her."

I pause for a moment, trying to wrap my mind around what Snabe just said. "Braco the motorcycle? You're talking about *Dellatrix's friend*, Braco. You're talking about your ex?" I yell. "Why the hell was she coming to see you in the first place?"

Bumbleborn's eyes go wide when he hears this, but he says nothing.

"Harriet, you knew she was still on the island," Snabe continues, trying desperately to calm me down. "She's getting off chocolate milk just like me. She has no idea where Dellatrix is and they were never really friends."

"I just…" I stammer. "I don't know how to react to this."

"I'm sorry," Snabe continues, struggling to clarify. "I know it's a little odd, but this is kinda perfect when you think about it. Braco called me and asked if she could come to the show, so I told her to take the boat. I should have mentioned it but this just happened. She knows how to drive it. Do you?"

I hesitate. "No."

"Does Bumbleborn?" Snabe continues.

I turn to look at Bumbleborn. "Do you know how to drive a boat?"

"Do I look like I know how to drive a boat?" the mammoth scoffs, almost offended by the very question. "I grew up in Iowa. Hell no, I don't know how to drive a boat."

"Exactly," Snabe continues.

I take a deep breath and then let it out slowly, trying not to completely freak out. "Okay, yeah. Braco can take us."

"I'll call her," the parasaurolophus bard continues. "Head down to the dock as soon as you can. She'll meet you guys there."

WORDS ON THE WATER

12

By the time we get to the water, the midday sun has started its descent, turning the once blue sky a deep purple that will soon erupt with pinks and oranges like spills of colorful paint.

It's strange being here, forced back to a place that I swore I'd never return to. Still, thinking back on my few dramatic days here is better than the other, more terrifying thoughts that cloud my mind. I have no idea just how far Dellatrix is willing to go, but the sentient motorcycle's already made one indirect attempt on my life. The next time I see her, I'm guessing she's going to be even more forward.

I may be a big city girl, but I'm not sure if I'm ready to face down a motorbike whose hell bent on ending my life, especially in this condition.

Bumbleborn drives down past the old cabins and parks so that we're right next to the beach. "Everything's gonna be okay," the mammoth assures me. "I've got you covered, and when we get to Dublin you and Snabe can figure out where to go from there."

"Thank you," tell him, genuinely appreciative of the kind words. It's not nearly enough to settle the nervous anxiety that's running wild through my body, but it's a start.

Bumbleborn and me climb out of the car to see Braco rolling down the road towards us, a confused look on her face.

"Harriet! Are you alright?" she asks, trying to focus on me but unable to keep her eyes from springing back up to Bumbleborn over and over again.

"Not really," I confess.

Braco opens up her arms wide and gives me a warm embrace, something that I never would've imagined happening between us. Strangely, it feels really nice, like a moment of true forgiveness.

Braco still hasn't stopped sneaking glances at the giant mammoth next to me.

"So… who is this?" the stark blonde machine finally asks, nodding towards the hulking dinosaur.

"Bumbleborn," the burly man replies, reaching out his large claw and giving Braco a firm shake.

"Are you dropping Harriet off?" Braco continues, confused.

Bumbleborn shakes his head. "I'm not leaving her side."

"Is that okay with Snabe?" Braco continues, awkward and nervous.

Honestly, I don't really blame her. I've quickly come to see Bumbleborn as a lovable friend, but without actually knowing the woolly mammoth's true disposition, he'd probably come across as absolutely terrifying. All of this talk about stalkers and threats just makes the whole thing even more intimidating, all kinds of moving parts that nobody seems to fully have a grasp on yet.

"Snabe's the one who sent him," I explain to Braco. "So yes, he's okay with it."

"I don't…" Braco begins, then trails off. The living motorcycle glances back over her should at the massive yacht lashed up on the dock below.

I follow her gaze, taking in the boat as it sways with the gentle evening breeze.

"I just didn't realize you'd have someone with you," Braco finally admits. "Do you really think that's necessary? Dellatrix's just making threats, she's not *really* gonna try to hurt you."

"She already did," I counter. "She tried to kill me, actually."

Braco seems completely taken off guard by this. "Wait what?"

I realize now that Snabe hasn't given her the full story, something we agreed to keep to ourselves but I'd promptly forgotten about.

"Dellatrix cut the breaks on Snabe's car," I continue. "We could've died."

Braco's just staring at me now with a blank expression on her face. She looks like a computer that's hit an error message, the information supplied simply too confusing or contradictory to process.

"I thought she just threatened you," the motorcycle finally blurts. "I mean, that's what Snabe said when he called me."

"It's more than just threats," I continue. "Dellatrix is utterly insane."

"And the longer we stand here, the more time she has to find us," Bumbleborn interjects. "So let's get going."

The hulking man opens up the back seat and grabs my bag, a small backpack with a weekend's worth of clothes that he drapes over his shoulder. I've also got my laptop and parchments in there, hoping to put the finishing touches on my spell once we extract ourselves from this drama.

Braco leads the way, strolling down the beach stairs and then heading out onto the dock. Bumbleborn and me follow closely behind, our senses heightened.

My new mammoth bodyguard is diligent with his work, keeping his eyes locked on the hillside behind us, and his hairy hand positioned just inches from his wand.

Braco climbs onto the boat first and then reaches out for my bag, which I toss over to her. The woman carries my luggage to the door of the boat's cabin, opening it a crack and then tossing my bag into the darkness beyond. My wand is in there, but with Bumbleborn by my side I'm not too worried about it.

Braco stands back up and then takes her position at the steering wheel, gazing off into the swiftly darkening horizon. "It's a two-hour ride," she says, "but the water's calm and we've got a little extra time regardless. I don't think we'll have any problem making it to the show before Snabe goes on."

The woman glances over at Bumbleborn, who's still on the dock.

"Can you untie those?" she questions, pointing over at the ropes that are wrapped tightly around the dock's metal handles.

Bumbleborn does as he's told, not wasting any time as he begins to unwind the thick rope. Eventually, he finishes and tosses the rope aboard, then quickly climbs on after it.

"And we're off," Braco says, returning to her position in front of the steering wheel. She begins to gradually pull back the throttle, sending our vessel faster and faster out into the vast blue ocean beyond.

The second we depart, I feel a beautiful wave of relief was over me, thankful to be away from that cove that has so darkly influenced my emotions and decisions. It's like a spell has been broken, the anxiety and fear slowly melting away over every passing second until it's completely drained.

I didn't create such an amazing life for myself just to have Dellatrix steal it away from me.

As Braco continues to man the steering wheel, I stroll over to Bumbleborn and sit down across from him at the back of the boat. It's loud out here, but not so bad that the two of us can't have a conversation. Bumbleborn's already used to shouting over loud rock and roll shows.

"Thank you," I tell him. "You're a good friend to Snabe, and now you're a good friend to me."

"Not a problem," Bumbleborn replies with a smile. "That's what I'm here for."

I glance back over at Braco, whose focus is locked squarely on the water before us. "Do you trust her?"

Bumbleborn shakes his head. "Not really, but I don't trust anyone. I understand why she's still around, though. It's hard for Snabe to give up on people that are making an effort to change. I think he sees himself in their struggle."

"I get that," I reply with a nod. "I just… I hope he's right about her."

It's dangerous to go out this late on the water without proper equipment, but luckily Snabe's customized yacht is set up with all the lighting gear we'll need to get to Dublin after dark.

I take a deep breath and stare out across the vast ocean, the sky now fully blossomed into a brilliant purple and orange sunset that seems to overwhelm everything. The rest of the islands in this chain dot the horizon line with massive black curves, humps that bubble up from the water on every side like enormous sea serpents.

It's the first time I've ever been this far out on a boat, and I suddenly begin to notice the pockets of floating debris that drift this way and that through the rocking waves nearby. There's not too much of the stuff, but every once in a while you'll catch sight of some driftwood that's been tangled together in the currents, trapped in a never ending cycle as it moves back and forth between the islands but never finds a place to land.

I wonder how long these logs have been out here, thinking back on stories of bottled messages that drifted in the sea for twenty or thirty years.

It's strange to imagine something floating for that long, over that many miles, just to come back and find itself in the arms of another human being who just happened to be strolling down the beach at the exact right moment.

The tides and currents have so much variation that it's impossible to calculate, but it's fun to picture them with a life of their own, a sentient, supernatural force carrying everything to its rightful destination; sometimes right away, and sometimes taking its sweet time.

Funny enough, it's that energy of fate that I tapped into to craft my new spell. I wanted to create something power, yet abstract, a spell that performs an action so simple, yet providing so much variation. To bend the hands of fate and put you exactly where you need to be at just the right time.

Sometimes that means finding your car keys before you head out to work. Sometimes that means traveling across the world to a cabin and finding your soul mate next door.

Sometimes that means a bottle on the water drifting exactly where it needs to be read.

Years ago I'd say this was an impossible magical feat, too strange, too undefined, if it weren't for that fact that I met Snabe through a swirling tide of my own, a life that was begging for direction and struggling against the rip tide that was pulling me down. This magical energy is out there, it's just waiting to be harnessed.

And harness it I did. I'm in the best relationship of my life. Even though Snabe is a complicated man, he fits me like a perfect puzzle piece. We're two gnarled hunks of driftwood that have tangled together in the waves, just thankful to be on this journey together.

I glance over at Bumbleborn, whose focus is elsewhere. The large mammoth continues to sit quietly, staring out at the glorious sky from his seat at the edge of the boat.

"I'm really excited for the show," I call over him, the fear that once overwhelmed me now a distant afterthought.

Bumbleborn smiles at me and opens his mouth to speak, but suddenly the prehistoric creature's expression changes as his eyes glance upward slightly, locked onto something over my shoulder. I don't even have time to glance back before there's a loud blast of magical energy and flame, a bolt launching across my field of vision and slamming Bumbleborn in the chest.

Immediately, bright red blood starts to surge out through the mammoth's fingers, spilling down the front of his shirt in a horrific, crimson waterfall. Dark magic swirls around him, drifting off of this new wound in toxic vapors.

The second Bumbleborn realizes what's happened he starts to fumble for his wand, but by then it's already too late. The mammoth falls forward and slams hard against the deck, his body completely ridged.

I spin around to find Dellatrix standing with her arm outstretched and a beginners wand held tight, a wild look in her eyes, which are bright red from an endless supply of sleepless nights and streaming tears. Most wands are only of use to seasoned wizards, but there are a few whose functions have been dumbed down into a single spell of aggression, sold back and forth on the wizard black market. They're unreliable, especially in the hands of an amateur, but they get the job done.

Dellatrix's hair is a wild mess, hanging down around her face is greasy dark strands. The motorcycle's makeup is smeared and bizarre, as though she's been applying it over and over again after every cry without going back to clean up the mess.

"What the fuck are you doing?" Braco screams from behind Dellatrix, her eyes just as wide as mine. "What the fuck?"

Dellatrix levels her wand at me, turning her head and shouting back to Braco. "Slow the boat down."

Braco is too flustered to follow any instructions at the moment, trembling with fear. I can see her repeating something to herself over and over again, the words furiously bubbling up over her lips in relative silence as she tries to make sense of the mammoth body pooling blood across the deck before her.

"Slow the boat!" Dellatrix screams again, the motorbike's expression hauntingly bizarre. Of course, I'd recognize this terrible machine anywhere, but there's something about her mannerisms that's just the slightest bit off. She looks like she's been gazing into the endless cosmic Void for far too long.

Obsession can really do a number on you, I realize.

Braco finally does as she's told, slowing the boat to a crawl.

"Surprise," Dellatrix offers with a smile, the motorcycle giving me a deeply unsettling wink.

"You said you were just going to scare her," Braco finally gets the courage to shout.

Dellatrix laughs. "Well, she looks pretty scared to me."

"You just *shot* someone!" Braco screams. "You murdered a dinosaur!"

"I didn't say anything about just scaring *him,*" Dellatrix replies.

"That's not... I don't..." Braco stammers, not quite sure how to reply. "Did you know he was coming?"

Dellatrix nods. "I figured he would."

"Why didn't you tell me?" Braco shrieks. "Oh my god! We're both going to jail!"

"No jail if there's no witnesses," Dellatrix replies.

The second I hear this my heart skips a beat. I have no idea what her plan is, but Dellatrix has clearly shown herself to be easily capable of violence. I'm utterly terrified, and the more time passes, the less likely I am to make it out of this situation alive. I need to think, to be utterly focused on the task at hand which, in this case, means survival.

My eyes begin to slowly make their way across my surroundings, carefully observing every little detail of the scene as it unfolds. Bumbleborn's wand is still resting somewhere under his large furry body, but because the ancient creature is lying face down on the ground, the prospect of getting to it quick enough is out of the question.

Meanwhile, my wand is stuffed into my bag in the main cabin.

There's a net attached to the side of the boat, well within reach, but the straps that hold it in place are confusing and well secured. It's doubtful I could quickly retrieve it, and even if I did, the thing appears to be made of soft aluminum. It's not *nearly* strong enough to serve as a weapon on its own.

Finally, I turn my powers of observation on Dellatrix and Braco themselves, relying on my wizardly attunement to the threads of reality to extrapolate their next moves.

Braco clearly didn't know what she was getting herself into when she agreed to whatever this is. As far as I know, Snabe has maintained his promise about keeping the worst of the threats under wraps, meaning Braco could've easily assumed this trip was an excuse for some harmless razzing. Maybe she thought they were gonna drop me off on one of the empty islands for a night, or just pretend they'd hurt me if I didn't leave town and never look back.

Lying at my feet, Bumbleborn suddenly groans.

"Oh thank god," Braco gushes. "He's still alive."

"Don't get too excited, he's got a wand," Dellatrix counters, then lifts her own magic stick and points it directly at Bumbleborn's back.

The mammoth remains motionless, sprawled out and bleeding on the boat's deck.

"Wait, wait!" Braco cries, waving her hands in the air. "Don't shoot him. I'll get his wand."

The frazzled blonde motorcycle rolls over to Bumbleborn, her eyes meeting mine for a fleeting moment and then drifting away. Despite its briefness, however, this visual exchange says a lot, a quick yet feeble apology for the situation we've both been thrust into. She says this without any words, but I know we can both feel it.

Braco searches around under Bumbleborn's body for a moment and then finds the wand, extracting it slowly before standing up once more. Her eyes remain lowered, however, focused on the weight of the magic stick as it rests in her hands.

"Throw it overboard," Dellatrix commands.

Braco hesitates. She turns around to face Dellatrix, but the wand remains tightly gripped within her hand.

I realize now that this could be my only chance, praying that Braco does the right thing.

"Do it," I mutter under my breath.

Dellatrix immediately turns her attention, and her wand, back towards me. "Don't you dare say another word."

Braco takes a deep breath, but still refuses to dispose of her magical weapon.

"Throw that wand over the side," Braco demands again.

Braco closes her eyes, waiting just a moment longer before finally tossing Bumbleborn's wand over the side of the boat with a meek splash. All of my hope is now quickly plummeting to the bottom of the ocean.

"Thanks," Dellatrix says with a sweet smile. "I'm sorry. You're making this really hard on me, but it only works if Snabe thinks *you* were the stalker."

The motorcycle raises her wand and shouts out a staccato incantation, firing three bolts of dark magical energy into Braco. The motorcycle cries and wobbles a bit, then tumbles to the deck. Soon, the pool of motor oil begins to grow even bigger across the yacht's stark white floor.

Dellatrix now turns her wand towards me.

"Don't!" I suddenly blurt, all that I can think to say. "You can't just kill me like this."

Dellatrix grins, finding this comment to be incredibly humorous for some reason. "Oh no, I'm not going to shoot you. Do you realize how long I've wanted to be with Snabe Rezmor? How many years I followed that band of bards around on the road, going to every show? Buying every shirt? My entire life revolved around that dinosaur before I even met him, and when we finally *did* meet it was the single most important thing that's ever happened to me."

"I didn't realize you were so... in love with him," I reply, trying desperately to appear supportive in some strange way.

Unfortunately, my words seem to have to opposite effect. "Didn't realize?" the motorcycle screams. "Are you kidding me? What we had was perfect before you showed up! The love we had is something you will never, ever understand!"

"You're right," I stammer. "I won't."

Dellatrix's expression twitches slightly as I say this, reacting to my words in a way that she didn't quite expect. She deeply enjoyed hearing it.

"For all the torture you've put me though," Dellatrix continues. "You don't deserve to be blasted with a magic bolt. You deserve to be dragged down into the deep, dark, ice cold ocean, struggling to break free like I struggle every day that me and Snabe are apart."

Dellatrix keeps her wand squarely pointed at my head, then slowly begins to back away. When she reaches the door of the boat's cabin, she opens it up and reaches inside, slowly dragging forth what appears to be a heavy, weighted fishing net.

"You really think this is gonna make Snabe want to be with you again?" I stammer, growing desperate. "You think he's gonna want to be with a killer?"

"Braco's the killer, remember? After all, they'll find tire tracks everywhere," the motorcycle informs me. "Sure, it might take a while, but eventually Snabe will try to move past all this tragedy with a little mindless love from a familiar body."

I don't want to give any credit to Dellatrix's absurd prediction, but the longer I allow her words to simmer in my mind, the more I start to realize that she might be right. As a romance bad boy at the end of his novel,

Snabe has been making good choices at every turn, but something this traumatic could easily send him back over the edge of self-destruction.

Braco drags the weighted net over and throws it to the ground before me, the massive pool of blood now soaking into its thick, rope threading. The thing is heavy enough to sink on its own, but it appears the edges are also lined with heavy metallic ball weights.

"Back over to the edge of the boat," Dellatrix commands.

I do as I'm told, my mind racing a mile a minute for anything that could possibly help me escape from this incredibly dire situation. Realizing there's not much time left, I consider going for the wand in Dellatrix's hand, but deep down I know that any attempt to disarm her is utterly futile. She's way too focused, carrying out a plan that's been running through her head over and over again for weeks now.

If only there was something unexpected that could turn things sideways, even for only a moment.

Suddenly, it hits me. My mind draws back to the beautiful evening when I first exchanged words with Snabe on this very boat.

I slowly creep my hand down into my pocket, my eyes remaining steady on Dellatrix but my thoughts elsewhere. I know that I'll only have one chance at this, and I need to be ready.

Unfortunately, things don't quite go as smoothly as I hoped.

Dellatrix laughs. "I can see what you're doing," she tells me. "You're not gonna call the police out here, there's no service on the water for miles and miles, and without a wand there's no magic flares to send up."

I let out a long sigh, retracting my phone from my pocket slowly. "You got me," I offer.

I find what I'm looking for, then hover my finger over the button.

"Why don't you throw that in the water, too?" Dellatrix suggests. "You'll need both hands to pull the net up over yourself."

"Okay," I offer with a smile.

I press the button.

My Bluetooth is still connected.

Suddenly, earsplittingly loud music erupts through the boat at an almost unfathomable volume, the same volume that Snabe had it pinned to when showing me his speakers some weeks ago. It's nearly enough to knock someone off their feet if they're not ready for it, the bass rumbling across our bodies in powerful waves.

Dellatrix flinches and the wand fires a single magical bolt, but it's now cocked at an angle as the motorcycle instinctively tries to cover her ears, a single blast of dark energy sailing off into the sky above.

Seizing my opportunity, I lunge at the motorbike, recalling every New York street fight I'd ever had in my youth. I swing my fist hard, hitting her in the face and knocking her backwards.

Dellatrix whips the wand around but I see it coming, immediately grabbing her before she can get her magical weapon aligned with my body. A second bolt erupts from the wand, but the music is blaring so loudly that I can barely hear the blast, recognizing it instead by the brilliant flash near the side of my head.

I shake the hand with the wand as hard as I can, trying to release Dellatrix's grip but unable to do so. She's thrashing about and screaming, revving her engine loudly as smoke begins to plume from her machinal body.

Suddenly, I stumble backwards, my feet caught up in the thick netting that covers the ground. The motorcycle comes with me, finally releasing her grip on the wand as it goes sliding across the blood soaked deck.

Unfortunately, Dellatrix still has the upper hand, and in my disorientation she manages to grab the net in her and throw it up over the top of my already tangled body.

Above us, the words "over the top of my already tangled body" appear, floating as a reaction to this spellsong in a haze of luminous neon.

In a normal scuffle, we'd find ourselves around the same strength, but now that I'm covered in heavy rope there's nothing I can do. My previous car crash injury isn't doing me any favors, either.

Belligerent with rage, the motorcycle pushes me farther and farther back until I hit the side of the boat, then farther still as she bends me over the edge. I'm tumbling backwards, hanging down so far that my hair is adrift in the icy cold water.

Below me is utter darkness.

Above, Dellatrix is shrieking out two words over and over again, but I can't quite hear them over the thundering music. For a brief second I can clearly see her lips, however, finally understanding.

"He's mine," Dellatrix screams in a crazed mantra, the words suddenly physically manifesting themselves everywhere around us.

My hands are gripped as tightly as they can to the edge of the boat, but

I'm quickly starting to realize I have little time left. With no other options, all that I can do is feel my fingers slowly uncurl, my body pushed closer and closer into the watery depths.

This is the end.

In this moment, I can't help wishing I'd spent more time on my goodbyes to Snabe; on my goodbyes to anyone, for that matter. It's crazy to think that, at some point in the future, you'll have your last interactions with the people you love. We always expect that day to come at some undefined future point, but then one day you wake up and there it is staring you right in the face.

I want to fight this, to find some way around the fate that's befallen me, but my options have gradually gone from limited to utterly hopeless. I've got nothing to grab onto, no way of fighting back, and no chance of survival once I'm in the water.

It's in these last moments that I notice something bobbing through the waves a few feet from my head, a piece of driftwood that's been cruising through these currents for weeks, months, or maybe even years. It's traveled far and wide, just to end up right here when I needed it the most.

There's a tingling in my fingertips, the same that I get when I'm casting with my wand and yet, at this point, there's no wand to be found. I'm not sure what to make of it, but there's definitely magic afoot. Maybe a ritual that was performed long ago and is finally coming to fruition.

My plan is a long shot, but at this point it's my only option. To reach out and grab the wood I'll need to release my grip with one hand, and at that point I'll only have a few seconds before tumbling overboard completely.

I make my choice.

As fast as I possibly can, I let go of the boat and reach back behind my head, frantically grasping in the cold black water. My hand wraps tight around something hard and wooden, and with all of my strength I heave it towards Dellatrix in a powerful overhead swing.

There is a loud crack as my wooden staff slams hard against Dellatrix's head, causing her to tumble back and release the net.

I don't stop for a second, immediately sitting up and continuing towards the dazed and disoriented motorcycle. I swing at her again, sending her reeling as motor oil spills everywhere. In her desperation to get away Dellatrix suddenly hits the gas, hard. The next thing I know, she's shooting past me and launching over the edge of the yacht.

The sentient motorcycle flies through the center of the phrase "flies through the center" hurled through the middle of the O and then landing in the dark water with a great splash.

I stand in utter shock, catching my breath as I struggle to make sense of what just happened. Slowly, my gaze drifts over to the long piece of driftwood in my hand, my eyes going wide when I realize that it's not actually driftwood at all, but the paddle of an old dingy.

I turn the oar over in my hand in utter disbelief.

Is it really possible? Could this be the paddle from our beach? Could fate have allowed some inconspicuous piece of wood to finally finish the job that it started?

Suddenly, I remember the spell that I'd been struggling with for months. This whole time I'd assumed it wasn't working quite right, but maybe it just takes its time to deliver. This is the hand of fate reaching out just like I'd asked. Maybe that day on the deck, when my wand let out the slightest fizzle of magical energy, wasn't a mistake after all.

I tossed this oar in the water on that beach long ago and, against all odds, it finally returned.

I reach into my pocket again and find my phone, pressing pause on the outrageously loud music that's been assaulting my eardrums this whole time. The silence that follows is absolutely glorious.

Suddenly, I remember Dellatrix and hurry to the edge of the boat, gazing out into the jet-black ocean in an effort to spot her floating body. I hate this woman with every ounce of my being, but despite everything she's done tonight, I can't just let her drown.

It seems the decision has been made for me, however. No matter how hard I try, I just can't seem to find her body floating in the salty waves. If she was a human then maybe things would be different, but motorcycles are heavy.   She's gone.

Below me, Bumbleborn lets out another long groan.

"Don't worry," I say, kneeling down next to the mammoth. "We're gonna get you help."

I stand up and head for the steering wheel, hoping to make sense of the controls.

Fortunately, it seems our loud music, glowing text and magical bolts of energy have alerted the Irish coastguard, whose bright lights shine out through the ever-looming darkness as they swiftly approach.

"Over here!" I call out, waving my arms despite the throbbing pain in my chest. "Help us!"

SEXUAL HEALING

13

Thankfully, this hospital is a lot bigger than the one on the island.

After a long ritual from some highly trained medical wizards and a brief knock on death's door, Bumbleborn appears to have stabilized. He's exhausted, of course, passed out in the hospital bed next to me, as I sit and stare out from the third story window at the faint lights of the city beyond. It's a beautiful night, and I'm so thankful I managed to stick around on this earth long enough to see it.

After everything that happened, we never did make it down to Dublin,

Instead, we ended up in the nearest port town the Irish coastguard could find; a little place called Bray. It's quaint, but apparently they know what they're doing when it comes to saving lives.

I glance over at Bumbleborn, his eyes closed tight as his massive woolly mammoth chest slowly heaves up and down. Looks like I'm the bodyguard now, I think to myself.

From the corner my eye, I catch a slight movement from the doorway. Fear strikes through my body, a natural reaction after the violent events that just transpired.

Fortunately, danger is still far, far away. It's exactly the person I want to see.

"Snabe," I murmur, the name falling heavy from my lips as I stand up and hurry across the room, throwing my arms around the parasaurolophus.

"I'm so sorry," he gushes, holding me close.

I let Snabe's warmth envelope my senses, allowing myself to enjoy every bit of safety and security that comes with it. It's been a long day walking on the razor's edge between life and death; all that I want now is comfort.

"I love you," I finally tell him, expelling the words I'd been praying for a chance to say.

Snabe pulls back for a moment, looking down at me with an excited and amused expression. He takes me in, our eyes locked. "I love you, too," he finally says.

Suddenly, we're kissing again, our lips meeting in a passionate embrace as tears begin to stream down the sides of my face.

From behind us, Bumbleborn clears his throat loudly.

Snabe and me release our grip on one another, turning to face the hospital bed in shock.

"Can't you do that somewhere else?" the mammoth groans mischievously. "I'm trying to sleep over here."

Snabe rushes over to the bed and sits down next to his friend. "You alright, mate?"

"Well, I got blasted with some nasty dark magic," Bumbleborn offers, "but thankfully Harriet was there to save me."

Snabe glances over his shoulder. "Was it Braco?"

I shake my head.

"Dellatrix?" he continues.

I nod. "They never found her body. She sunk like a rock."

Bumbleborn interjects, gruffly. "It's for the better."

I decline to comment.

"I'm glad you're okay," Snabe tells his injured friend.

"I'm fine, I'm fine," Bumbleborn continues. "How was the show?"

"It was... good. Really good," the love of my life offers. Snabe glances up at me as he says this, and I smile.

"I wish I could've seen it," I tell him.

"They'll be more," the bard states with absolute confidence.

Bumbleborn closes his eyes, a half smile still plastered across his face. "Well, wake me up when that happens. Until then, get the hell out of here."

Snabe laughs and then strolls back over to me. "How about it?" my parasaurolophus lover questions. "You wanna get the hell out of here?"

I nod.

The two of us turn and leave, heading out down a long, sterile hallway that is completely empty at this late hour.

We don't get far before Snabe stops us. "I really am sorry," he says, turning to me with a look of deep sincerity on his face. "I've been trying to make good choices, but I failed you. I should've cut that part of my life out entirely. Trusting Braco was so, so stupid."

I shake my head. "She wasn't trying to hurt us," I explain. "She just didn't know any better."

Snabe takes a deep breath. "Still, I'm sorry. I'm gonna do everything that I can to make it up to you."

"Promise?" I coo playfully.

Snabe nods. "It's the end of the book so… yeah… you can trust me."

"Let's get started then" I reply, pushing the hulking dinosaur backwards through the doorway of an empty hospital room.

I'll admit, being this aroused after such a harrowing ordeal seems a little unexpected, but there's something about nearly losing your life that makes you truly appreciate what little time you have. I want Snabe, and I'm not interested in waiting.

I want that connection; to feel his scaly dinosaur body against mine as we fall into perfect sync with one another.

We continue to feverishly kiss until Snabe's yellow eyes drift up to the security camera hanging above us. Even though this wing of the hospital appears to be relatively empty, there are eyes everywhere.

Snabe begins to hum a little tune, growing louder and louder with his magical song until, suddenly, the cameras erupt in a shower of sparks, completely fried.

"I so jealous you bards don't need wands," I gush, pulling him close again and running my hands excitedly across the dinosaur's incredible, toned abs. I begin to kiss his chest, moving my way lower and lower across Snabe's perfect physique. I start to undo Snabe's belt but he stops me suddenly.

"I'm making it up to *you*," he reminds me. "Not the other way around."

Snabe takes control now, pushing me back so that I'm sitting on the bed with my legs spread slightly. The handsome parasaurolophus unbuttons my jeans and strips them away from my skin, exposing my bare legs to the cool air.

He reaches up and takes ahold of my panties next, slowly sliding them down as my arousal reaches its absolute peak. I am aching for his touch, craving it like nothing I've ever desired before.

Fortunately, Snabe doesn't make me wait long. The dinosaur grabs me with his muscular arms a pulls me over to the edge of the bed, then climbs down onto his knees before me. He looks up and smiles, then dives in hungrily.

"Oh fuck," I groan, leaning back and opening up my legs even more, giving my man some space to work.

Snabe begins to suck me slowly, taking his time with my body yet somehow knowing exactly when to change the pace. Eventually, Snabe will speed up, but quickly pulls back before I have a chance to travel too far down this path of sensations.

It sounds like this could get irritating quickly, but the result is far, far from it. Instead of growing frustrated, I find myself excited for what comes next, taken on a journey through every subtle step of my blossoming pleasure.

Snabe continues to work me for a long while, my stomach clenching and releasing with spastic movements of excitement.

"I thought I was gonna lose everything," I finally groan. "I thought I was gonna lose *you*."

Snabe stops pumping his head up and down for a moment and looks up. "I'm right here," he assures me.

"Come on," I coo. "I need you closer."

The breathtakingly handsome dinosaur stands and undoes his belt, slipping out from the last of his clothes as he climbs onto the bed with me. I pull my legs back and Snabe's muscular torso slips between, his enormous cock pushing up into me at just the right angle.

I let out a startled whimper as Snabe enters my pussy, not entirely prepared for his enormous size but gradually growing accustomed to his girth. What begins as a slight discomfort soon evolves into a pleasant warmth, blossoming deep down in the pit of my stomach.

I wrap my arms around the parasaurolophus's enormous frame, pulling him close as he heaves against me. I'm breathing deep, appreciating every bit of sensation as my body is flooded by a myriad of feelings. It's a lot to keep up with, but I'm trying my best to feel them all, to appreciate this beautiful moment for exactly what it is.

Soon enough, Snabe and me have found a steady rhythm together, our bodies rocking back and forth like a single sexual entity. The pleasure that flows between us has created some sort of feedback loop that I cannot fully grasp or understand, but I've never been more thankful to be a part of it.

This pressure within me continues to build and build, causing my body to tremble wildly beneath Snabe. It feels as though I could explode in a blissed out orgasm at any moment.

I reach down and begin to get myself off in time with the dinosaur's movements, pumping my hand furiously.

"I love you so much," Snabe tells me.

Before I have a chance to reply, the sensations of climax erupt through my being, spilling out down my arms and legs in a potent blast of electricity and endorphins. I feel as though I've left my body, momentarily outside of myself as the potent feelings become just too overwhelming to maintain.

"Oh my god," I'm screaming.

The orgasm seems like it will last forever, but eventually I find myself returning to this layer of reality. Snabe has finished, as well, but he stays within me for a moment, taking his time as he kisses me softly.

Eventually, the two of us disconnect and begin to pull on our clothes.

"Hey!" a doctor suddenly shouts from the doorway. "What are you doing in here?"

Snabe turns to him and smirks. "What does it look like?"

"You have to leave," the doctor informs us, sternly.

I can't help but chuckle to myself over Snabe's nonchalance in the face of this very disgruntled man.

I guess no matter what happens, he's always gonna be a bit of a bad boy.

BILLINGS

14

The second the lights go down, this entire arena full of fans erupts into an earsplitting cheer, so loud that the sound begins to transform and distort, becoming more akin to the roar of a single massive beast than the shrieks of several thousand distinct people.

Four vague shadows make their way out onto the stage, shrouded in darkness but just visible enough to make the audience strain their voices even louder.

Moments later, a low rumbling bass tone fills the massive room, vibrating through my body from the ground up.

I'm standing on the side of the stage, just a few feet off of the wings with various crewmembers and super fans by my side. It's the best seat in the house, and I still haven't grown tired of it after two weeks on the road with the dinosaur of my dreams.

Suddenly, a powerful guitar chord surges through the arena, light simultaneously blasting outward with a brilliant yellow glow. I can see nothing but excited faces across the first few rows, wide smiles and joyful eyes of anticipation now illuminated. This moment means so much to them, and they are fully here for it, completely appreciating every passing second.

I'd like to think I'm on this level too these days. At least, I'm trying my best.

The songspell kicks in as suddenly everything explodes with brilliant radiance, the band prowling the stage as magical plumes of color dance through the air, taking the shape of physically manifested text that reads from this very book. Snabe is out front, the leader of the pack who immediately seizes control of the situation. Before him, an audience of several thousand fans are completely under his metamagic spell, caught up in the moment before they can even grasp what's happening.

Now, everyone is singing along to this powerful mantra, belting out the words as if their life depended on it.

I recognize this song. It's the track that played out from my phone that fateful day on the water.

This song saved my life.

There's a quick break in the vocals and Snabe glances over at me, making eye contact and smiling wide as he sees me rocking out to the music. I give him a playful wink and he nods in return, then turns back to the roaring crowd before kicking into the next verse.

The parasaurolophus reaches down and grabs his shirt, pulling it up over his head and tossing it out into the frantic screaming masses. His chest and abs look absolutely majestic tonight under the brilliant stage lights.

I roll my eyes, but I also kinda love it.

"He normally saves the shirt thing until song three or four, doesn't he?" Minerma asks, stepping up next to me.

"Yep," I reply with a nod. "Guess it's just one of those nights."

My spellcrafting agent laughs and puts her arm around my shoulder in a brief hug. "I've gotta say, this is by far the most entertaining bard tour I've ever been allowed to tag along on."

"Not everyone gets to do one signing at a magic store in the afternoon and then another at a bard show in the evening," I tell her.

"No they certainly don't," Minerma replies, shaking her head in amazement.

"Sales good?" I question, turning to my friend.

"You're literally on track to be our company's all-time biggest seller for the second time," Minerma reminds me. "So yeah, sales are good. You should almost get drowned by angry motorcycles more often."

My eyes go wide at this shockingly edgy joke from my otherwise strait-laced agent. "Minerma! That's not funny!"

Minerma shrugs. "Fuck it."

I can't help myself, I actually laugh.

"Looks like it's good for album sales, too," Minerma continues, nodding out towards the crowd.

The song finishes and Snabe steps forward a bit, walking out to the edge of the stage as a soft spotlight envelopes him. "How's everyone doing tonight?" the beautiful, tattooed parasaurolophus calls out.

The crowd roars in response.

"Good," Snabe replies with a smile. "Me too. Listen, we normally save this song until the end, but I'm just too excited about it, so I think we're gonna play it now. Is that okay with you guys?"

Once more, the crowd erupts in a raucous cheer.

I'm utterly confused by all this, not exactly sure what's happening. Seven Inch Nails put on an incredible show every night, but it's also a show that never changes, strictly planned out down to the last second. I could tell you the song order in my sleep, and this is the first time since the start of the tour that they've deviated.

Snabe turns around and strolls over to the side of the stage where I'm standing. He's grinning wide, clearly amused by my state of bewilderment.

"Come on," the handsome dinosaur bard offers, extending his hand.

"What are you doing?" I question.

"Singing your song," he informs me.

I laugh and then finally give in, allowing Snabe to take my hand in his claw as I follow him out under the warm lights of the stage. The second the crowd sees us together they completely lose their minds, reaching a previously unattained level of utter cacophony.

With my new wizard spell, and Snabe's bardic album, on the top of our respective charts, this reaction only makes sense. We're quickly turning into something of an *it* couple in the magic world, for better or worse, and just the sight of us holding hands is enough to send people into a rabid frenzy. It's a kind of fame that I've never experienced, and although I'm still having trouble getting used to it, it's certainly not bad.

There are much worse positions to be in.

I see now that the stagehands have brought a stool out onto the stage. Typically, this is where a performer might sit, but Snabe offers it to me with the gesture of his hand.

"Really?" I question.

Snabe nods and I take a seat, then he turns to address the audience once more. "There was a time when Harriet Porber didn't like me very

146

much, and with good reason," he states, the dinosaur's amplified voice booming out across the packed arena. "As you know if you've read any tabloids over the last decade or so, I can be a bit of a cock."

The crowd cheers and I can't help chuckling to myself, slightly turning away out of embarrassment.

"I know, I know," Snabe says. "I'm working on it. Anyway, Harriet was a little upset with me, and I had this spell that I knew she liked. I'd been working on it for years, actually, but never quite knew how to finish it. Kinda like my shitty attitude, working on it for years, but something was never quite right. Harriet actually helped me figure out both of these problems, so this songspell is for her."

Of course, I know exactly what Snabe's going to play before he even starts. While previous versions of this little tune had been very sparse, the band is performing the fully realized arrangement now, complete with drums and bass. I prefer it stripped down, intimate style myself, but who am I to complain?

Snabe sings the song directly to me, walking around the stool that I sit on in playful circles as I watch with rapt attention. It's a meaningful moment, but also incredibly fun.

When the chorus finally hits, I can hear the crowd joining in behind Snabe with a massive wave of sound, singing along my name at the top of their lungs.

The arena momentarily disappears and for a brief second all of us understand how beautiful, unique and important we really are. We realize our place as characters on a journey who are better at being ourselves than anyone else is, and the cosmic power that comes with that. We fully grasp that sometimes our bodies and our souls are perfectly matched, and sometimes they're matched in a way that's uncomfortable, but these differences speak nothing to the purity and strength of the soul itself.

It's overwhelming, the sheer force of the sonic waves alone enough to make me tear up slightly.

Snabe sees this and comes in closer, kneeling down before the stool to comfort me, which just makes me cry even harder.

The song continues like this and I try my best to collect myself, but once the waterworks start flowing there's just no turning back. I'm not the hard ass I once was, and there's no hiding that now.

As the last chorus rolls around, I see something strange from the corner of my blurry, tear-filled eyes. I can barely make out several figures standing on the side of the stage, but a few of them gradually start to look familiar. In my emotional delirium, I think I can see my parents, and my sister, and my closest friends, all of them watching me from just off in the wings. It looks like they're crying too.

It's not until the last chord finally rings out that I realize my visions are real. Everyone I care about is here, for reasons that I can't quite wrap my head around just yet. Tonight's gig is in Billings, Montana, far from home.

When I turn my attention back to Snabe, I notice he's down on one knee before me, a wide smile plastered across his handsome face.

The crowd audibly gasps, their individual reactions heaping together in one powerful gust of sound.

"Harriet, will you marry me?" Snabe asks, his voice carrying out for miles.

I don't even hesitate. "Yes!" I tell him. "Of course!"

The crowd goes wild as Snabe erupts to his feet, wrapping me in his massive arms. He holds me close, the two of us surrounded by thousands but, for a brief moment, in our own private world.

In Snabe's arms, I feel like I'm free to love, free to relax, free to create. I feel safe to be me.

ABOUT THE AUTHOR

Dr. Chuck Tingle is an erotic author and Tae Kwon Do grandmaster (almost black belt) from Billings, Montana. After receiving his PhD at DeVry University in holistic massage, Chuck found himself fascinated by all things sensual, leading to his creation of the "tingler", a story so blissfully erotic that it cannot be experienced without eliciting a sharp tingle down the spine. Chuck's hobbies include backpacking, checkers and sport.

Made in the USA
Columbia, SC
25 August 2024

41159929R00087